MW01680615

Overlord

Nicholas Hagger is a philosopher, cultural historian, poet and former lecturer in Islam and Japan. He is a also a prolific author whose long-term project is to present the universe, world history and human life in terms of the mystic Fire or Light, the metaphysical vision that is central to his work.

By the same author

The Fire and the Stones
A Mystic Way
Selected Poems
A Smell of Leaves and Summer
A Spade Fresh With Mud
The Universe and the Light
The Warlords
A White Radiance

Overlord
Books 1–2

The Triumph of Light
1944–45

An Epic Poem

Nicholas Hagger

vega

First published by Element Books Ltd 1995

ISBN 1-84333-653-7

A catalogue record for this book is available from the British Library

Published in 2002 by
Vega
64 Brewery Road
London, N7 9NT

A member of Chrysalis Books plc

Visit our website at www.chrysalisbooks.co.uk

Printed in Great Britain
by Lightning Source
Cover designed by Design Revolution, Brighton

SUMMARY AND INDEX OF LINE NUMBERS

BOOK 1: EISENHOWER INVADES

BOOK 2: THE TYRANNICIDES FAIL

337-499	Christ's speech concerned at Hitler's genocide and atomic bomb programme and supporting Stauffenberg's bomb plot.
500-709	The seven Hells.
710-838	Satan's speech proposing an invasion of Heaven, support for Stalin and the enslavement of mankind.
839-870	Auschwitz.
871-950	Eisenhower visits Normandy.
951-982	Kay's return.
983-1013	German reaction to the war.
1014-1059	Montgomery attacks Caen.
1060-1174	Christ visits Heisenberg.
1175-1127	German Army plot.
1128-1271	God and evil.
1272-1307	Universe of love.
1308-1383	Hitler's evil within God's Fire.
1384-1423	Stauffenberg's knowledge of the Light through Stefan George.
1424-1463	Christ visits the plotters.
1464-1527	Rommel is strafed on Montgomery's orders.
1528-1571	Christ visits Stauffenberg in church on eve of plot.
1572-1774	Stauffenberg's attempt to kill Hitler in Rastenburg.
1775-1819	Hitler discovers the coup attempt during Mussolini's visit.
1820-2079	The failure of Stauffenberg's coup in Berlin, his arrest and execution.
2080-2104	Hitler's speech threatening a purge.
2105-2138	Divine perspective on Stauffenberg's action.
2139-2241	The two forces or laws in the universe, Light and Darkness, and their embodiment in Eisenhower-Stauffenberg and Hitler.

PREFACE
TO OVERLORD, BOOKS 1 AND 2

Epic is recognised by its: subject matter; theme; heroic tone; narrative length; complexity; unity of action; the scope of its setting; the scale of its action; the moral stature of its heroes; its supernatural elements; its conventions; its accessible language; its exact metre; and its distinctive cosmology.

An epic poem's subject matter includes familiar and traditional material drawn from history and widely known in popular culture, which reflects the civilisation that threw it up. Its theme has a historical, national, religious or legendary significance. It narrates continuously the heroic achievements of a distinguished historical, national or legendary hero or heroes at greater length than the heroic lay, and describes an important national enterprise in more realistic terms than fantastic medieval Arthurian (Grail) romance; it gives an overwhelming impression of nobility as heroes take part in an enterprise that is larger and more important than themselves. Its long narrative is characterised by its sheer size and weight; it includes several strands, and has largeness of concept. It treats one great complex action in heroic proportions and in an elevated style and tone. It has unity of action, which begins in the middle ("in medias res", to use Horace's phrase). The scope of its geographical setting is extensive, perhaps cosmic; its sweep is panoramic, and it uses heroic battle and extended journeying. The scale of the action is gigantic; it deals with good and evil on a huge scale. Consequently, its hero and main characters have great moral stature. It involves supernatural or religious beings in the action, and includes prophecy and the underworld. It has its own conventions; for example, it lists ships and genealogies, and the exploits that surround individual weapons. Its language is universally accessible, and includes ornamental similes and recurrent epithets. It uses exact metre (hexameters or the pentameters of blank verse). It has its own cosmology, and explains the ordering of the universe.

Homer's *Iliad*, which is about the Greeks' war against Troy, and Virgil's *Aeneid*, which is about the foundation of Rome, established the epic genre and defined these epic elements or components, and Milton's *Paradise Lost* conformed to them; while Dante's *Divine Comedy* and Ezra Pound's *Cantos* echo the lofty epic tone. My poem *Overlord*, the first two books of which I now offer, is about the liberation of Europe from tyranny and also reflects the characteristics of epic.

The subject matter of *Overlord* includes familiar and traditional historical material drawn from the Second World War, which has shaped the world of the last fifty years and reflects Western civilisation in a time of conflict, division and crisis. The Second World War is often referred to as an epic struggle, and is known to all people through living memory, books and films, regardless of age, wealth, position or social class; it has passed into popular culture. My theme, the liberation of Europe from Nazi tyranny, is of historical, national and legendary significance, and is still regarded as being of national importance in both the US and Europe. Eisenhower is a distinguished hero involved in a great complex action which has unity – the invasion of German-occupied France and the advance to Berlin – and he is involved in a noble enterprise of complexity and scope. *Overlord* begins with D-Day in June 1944 and narrates the American and British – and later, Russian – drive against Hitler, which ended with the fall of Berlin and led to the explosion of the atomic bomb. Book 2 narrates Stauffenberg's plot to kill Hitler.

A word about *Overlord's* narrative length. The massiveness of the theme of the Anglo-American triumph over Hitler following his conquest of and overlordship over Europe and his onslaught on the Jews and Christendom, requires *Overlord* to be of greater narrative length than past epics. Whereas Homer's twenty-four books tend to be around five hundred lines each and Virgil's and Milton's twelve books around a thousand, give or take a hundred or two, *Overlord's* first two epic books are respectively over 2,900 and 2,200 lines long; the events before and after D-Day, the bomb plot and their supernatural context simply cannot be done in less.

The scale of the action in *Overlord* derives from Hitler, who dwarfs all his predecessors in sheer awfulness and evil. To Marlowe, writing in the 1590s, the worst and cruellest military tyrant was the 14th century Timur Lenk, or Tamburlaine the Great. To Dostoevsky in *Crime and Punishment* and Tolstoy in *War and Peace* Napoleon was the most wicked man who could be imagined, a military tyrant who flouted all moral laws. On precise analysis, the Napoleonic Wars of 1800-1815 killed no more than half a million French people (one sixtieth of the French population at the time), and if we agree that Napoleon killed more of his enemies, then he was responsible for the deaths of between a million and a million and a half human beings in all, 0.43 per cent of mankind, which then totalled 1 billion (i.e. 1,000 million). The total dead in the First World War amounted to no more than eight and a half million, and according to the best studies Stalin is thought to have been responsible for killing 20 million. Census records recently discovered in the Kremlin show that Hitler's Operation Barbarossa resulted in 49 million Soviet dead alone (see *Barbarossa, The Axis and the Allies*, edited by John Erickson and David Dilks, pages 256-258), which puts up the conservative estimate of the total number of dead in World War Two from just under 36 million (including 18 million Russians) to 67 million, nearly 3.4 per cent of the total population of the world in 1939, which was 2 billion (or 2,000 million); and the higher estimate of 60 million dead to a staggering 90 million, or over 4.5 per cent of all mankind, nearly one in twenty human beings. Never in human history has one tyrant stood accused of being responsible for killing 67 million of his fellow humans, let alone 90 million. On a statistical count of the numbers of deaths and taking just the conservative figures into consideration, Hitler was almost forty-five times as bad as Napoleon, and nearly eight times as destructive as the entire First World War. He was responsible for killing more than three times as many people as the tyrants Stalin or Mao, and this is the context for the genocide he presided over, the liquidation of over 5.9 million out of the 8.86 million European Jews, one third of the world's Jewish population.

The heroes who resist tyranny have moral stature, and the larger the tyrant the greater their stature. In opposing the killer of at least 67 million people, the pragmatic Eisenhower and the idealistic Stauffenberg therefore take on an awesome moral and human stature. The moral choices take place in situations of everyday ordinariness, even banality, and the evidence for Eisenhower's strange affair with his driver is detailed in Kay Summersby Morgan's *Past Forgetting:*

My Love Affair with Dwight D. Eisenhower. Full accounts of the long influence of the poet Stefan George, whose poem *Antichrist* is about Hitler, on Stauffenberg's life can be found in Joachim Kramarz's *Stauffenberg* and Michael Baigent and Richard Leigh's *Secret Germany: Claus von Stauffenberg and the Mystical Crusade Against Hitler*.

In *Overlord* supernatural elements blend with history. Scenes of realistic everyday life take place within the context of the supernatural as the forces of Light and Darkness, personified by the Cosmic or universal Christ and Cosmic Satan in Heaven and Hell, attempt to influence the action on earth. (Yeats said we make art out of the quarrel with ourselves and rhetoric out of the quarrel with others, and my quarrel with myself is inextricably connected with this conflict, or quarrel, between Light and Darkness, and its Christian and Luciferian manifestations on earth, where genocidal dark forces such as the Illuminati and Nazis claim to follow the mystic Light.) Hitler's – and the Nazis' – interest in the occult and the influence of the poet Dietrich Eckart on Hitler are dealt with in a number of books, notably in Nicholas Goodrick-Clarke's *The Occult Roots of Nazism,* Nigel Pennick's *Hitler's Secret Sciences* and Dusty Sklar's *The Nazis and the Occult*. Hermann Rauschning, Governor of Danzig, hinted in *Hitler Speaks* (1939) that Hitler was possessed by the Devil, the Beast, and the circumstantial evidence for his Satanism is cited in such books as H. G. Baynes's *Germany Possessed (1941)*, Pauwels and Bergier's *The Morning of the Magicians*, Trevor Ravenscroft's *The Spear of Destiny* and Francis King's *Satan and Swastika: The Occult and the Nazi Party*.

Overlord connects Hitler's dark mania for destruction to the contemporary legend of the millennium and the Second Coming, and identifies the Battle of Normandy as the Battle of Armageddon which, under Satan's leadership, succeeds a thousand years of Christ's rule through the Holy Roman Empire during the time of nations, and precedes a thousand years of supra-national universal religion. In *Overlord* the Cosmic or universal Christ is endeavouring to set up a new universalist era which will express itself in a world government. Through Hitler, Satan is trying to set up his alternative millennial thousand year Reich. Like Michelangelo's vision on the Sistine Chapel ceiling, *Overlord* addresses and explores good and evil on a huge scale, and their origins in and connections with Heaven and Hell.

Eisenhower is the instrument for bringing in the universal Christ's world rule. Eisenhower will eventually be shown the new age, and will realise that although he is working for the defeat of Hitler in the short term, he is endeavouring to bring in a globalist world government. My universalist work of history, *The Fire and the Stones*, shows that such a world rule occurs in stage 15 of the 61 stages a civilisation goes through, that the North American civilisation is currently in this stage and that such a stage is always associated with epic. As well as marking the British contribution to victory, *Overlord* is a celebration of the rise of globalism within the American world-wide civilisation, and its hero Eisenhower is the figurehead in establishing the foundations for this US world rule, first on the battlefield in 1944-1945 and then as President of the US from 1953 to 1961.

Overlord adheres to the epic conventions. For example, a catalogue of Angels and demons echoes Homer's catalogue of ships, and the spear of Longinus is introduced within the context of a list of historical events with which it has been associated. The language of *Overlord* is accessible and includes ornamental similes.

Overlord uses strict metre. I eschew the Stress Metre that can be found in places in my *Collected Poems,* and use a blank verse that can be both elevated and descriptive. It has strictly five feet to a line, although an occasional effect requires an extra half-foot. My verse consists of iambic pentameters with occasional trochees and spondees, but no anapaests or dactyls, which I have employed in my two verse plays about the last year of the Second World War, *The Warlords*, Parts One and Two. Whereas spoken dramatic verse benefits from the loosening effects of anapaests and dactyls, epic poetry must be metrically tighter, variations being achieved in other ways than mixed metres. The one poetic licence permits some words to be scanned in either of two ways. Thus "Heaven", "seven", "driven", "General", "cruel" and "power", for example, can be scanned as one foot or as two; "Admiral", "areas", "Eisenhower", "genius", "Aetius", "history", "Aryan", "Emperor", "Catholic" and "several" can be scanned as two feet or as three; and "military" and "spiritual" can be scanned as three feet or as four. In all these cases, when the lower number is used the stresses of contemporary spoken English are allowed to override a strict syllabic count. On very rare occasions an elision is allowed, as in "the angelic".

Overlord has its own cosmology, and passages such as lines 182-315 give an account of the creation and ordering of the universe. As readers of *A Mystic Way* will know, I have had the idea for this epic since 1969 and I discussed it with Ezra Pound in Rapallo in 1970. I have put it off for over twenty-five years, until my vision had developed sufficiently to cope with the idea. The trouble was, existing philosophy could not encompass the cosmology of the Fire or Light, and so on the way I have had to found a new school in philosophy, Universalism. Now I can at last tackle this work, the starting-point of which is a unified vision of the universe, an understanding of the rise and fall of civilisations and of the laws of history, a sound grasp of where science and philosophy have gone wrong, a metaphysical perspective that includes the supernatural, and a knowledge of the laws by which the universe is run: the laws of the Light. My writings on mysticism, history, science, philosophy and metaphysical cosmology have been the perfect preparation for this daunting work, which revives the epic in our time and of which the following pages represent but the first sixth.

13th February 1995

~ BOOK 1 ~
EISENHOWER INVADES

Tell, Muse, of tyranny and millions killed,
Of the pinnacle of the world's power
Among mountain peaks and green slopes, of cruel
Destruction of cities, and whispers of
A Nazi atomic bomb. And tell of
The rise of Eisenhower and, with Christ's help,
The defiance of his supreme command
And opposition on the battlefield
Of Montgomery and Zhukov which led
To the liberation of Europe from
Nazi tyranny, the fall of Berlin
And the defeat and death of Hitler, who,
With counter-symmetry and chiasmus,
Plunged earthwards when he lost Satan's support
Like a falling star with a burning trail.
And tell of Light's triumph over Darkness
Though Satan's guile nearly outwitted Christ
Through his wily disciple, Stalin, and
Near spoilt God's plan for the millennium.

Tell, Muse, of plans and battles, commanders,
Of ambition and conflict, as the day
Of decision approached that would decide
Who would be Overlord of the whole world,
Whether Hitler, Overlord of Europe,
Commander-in-Chief of German armies
Whose genocidal rule of gun and noose
Conquered his neighbours in a new empire
Till tyrannicides challenged him, to bring
In a post-Nazi regime with Rommel
Or Beck as Head of State to end the war;
Or divine Hirohito, prisoner of
His murderous Army Generals, Overlord
Of Asia, Hitler's sole ally now that
Mussolini was gone; or Eisenhower,
Supreme Commander of Allied Forces,
The man who more than any other ran
The war and planned an Allied victory
And brought about American world rule;
Or Montgomery, implementer of
Operation Overlord; or Roosevelt

Or Truman, leaders of the world's foremost
Rising power; or proud Churchill, who still held
The British Empire that ruled a quarter
Of the colonial world, and who had stood
Alone when Europe fell and, brave, defied
The cruel dictators' might; or bland Marshal
Stalin, co-ordinator of Russian
Forces which were led by Marshal Zhukov,
Who sought world power for a land of peasants.
And tell, Muse, of the financiers behind,
Of plots among the Illuminati,
Those around Roosevelt who funded lend-lease,
Who paid the piper and then called the tune;
Tell of the betrayal of the good to
Establish Communism in Eastern
Europe, tell of destruction of cities
To further the interests of the few
Who would be Overlords, Olympians,
Of the world by the end of the century.
And tell, Muse, since all we know is One which
Includes both seen and unseen, of conflicts
Among the immortals in higher worlds,
Between the councils of Heaven and Hell
As God's representative, the Cosmic
Christ, the universal prophet, tussled
With Satan, who, in his more moderate
And deceptive form, Lucifer, wrought ill.
Tell, Muse, of the immortals' struggle to
Influence man, how Satan used his role
As deceiving Lucifer, "light-bearer",
To extend his domain, how, briefly, Christ
Despaired of saving Christendom, and wept.
Tell of great deeds and thoughts both above and
Below as the One divine Overlord –
Neither Father nor Mother, yet person,
A force of Love which can be more than "it" –
Prevailed through "its" good earthly counterpart
After the systematic destruction
Of men and cities, palaces, churches,
When the infernal Overlord appeared
To triumph through "its" earthly counterpart.
Justify evil in the highest good,
Tell how good prevailed to be hijacked by
Satan, and tell of the struggle for good
To triumph now in our new world order,

Tell how world government need not require
Wars, famines, plagues or genocide, but can
Bring peace, food, health and safety to mankind;
Tell how a universal Hell of slaves
Can become a universal concord
In a work that greets the millennium
As did Virgil's when Augustus's peace
Called all men to be Roman citizens.
Tell of eternal verities and tell
Of ultimate things, universal laws,
How divine Light shines into history,
How Providence moves civilisations,
The clash of monstrous egos and ideals,
Of barbarous tyranny and liberty,
Tell of the final triumph of the Light
In the smoke and blood of titanic wars.

O shades of my forerunners, o Homer
Who showed gods beside heroes on the plains
Of Troy; o Virgil, who told of the dark
Fortunes of Aeneas, both on earth and
In the underworld; o Romancers, who
Sang of the search for the Grail, the chalice
That shone with pure Light; o Dante, who with
Virgil passed from dark Hell to Paradise;
O Marlowe of the warlike Tamburlaine,
O Shakespeare of *Henry the Fourth* and *Fifth*;
O Donne, who judged the new philosophy
And science of a sceptical new Age,
And abandoned *The Progresse of the Soule*,
An epic work on the scale of nature
(From first apple to Queen Elizabeth);
O blind Milton, who lamented the lost
Paradise of Satan-Cromwell's England,
Who justified the ways of God to man;
O Marvell, whose Garden was Paradise;
O Dryden, who showed Monmouth's rebellion;
O Pope, whose sylphs guarded Belinda's lock;
O Goethe, whom Weishaupt called Abaris,
Who created Faust as illuminate;
O Blake, whose Hell was a great energy,
Who wrote of Milton and of higher worlds;
O Coleridge, who opposed Newton's mind
As passive, "mere materialist", and
Reconciled physics and metaphysics;

O Wordsworth, who pondered an epic on
King Arthur and, listless, recoiled and drooped;
O Shelley, who revealed the One as Light;
O Tennyson, who wrote of Arthur's wars;
O Hardy, who recreated the wars
Of Napoleon – I beg you, help me.
O Pound, who saw the decline of the West
And hinted at a deeper meaning, you
Who sat under a Rapallo full moon
And urged me to begin this task which I
Have now pushed aside for twenty-five years,
Who stood and gripped my hand, passed on the power
Of Calliope's art – I salute you.
And all who wrote of the great battles of
History: Troy, Actium, the Spanish
Armada, Trafalgar, Waterloo and
The Somme; as I gaze at a hedge I see
I grow a white vision like a wild plant –
Please come to my aid with heroic verse
In twelve books like twelve leaves on the stem of
Jack-by-the-hedge (garlic mustard) which grows
Wild in hedgerows and ends in a white flower.

Tell, Muse, how the Allies waited to sail.
Just as Agamemnon surveyed the fleet
Of the Greeks that would face Trojan Priam,
And felt the loneliness of leadership,
Responsibility of sole command,
So, hands in pockets, jaw thrust out at wind,
General Eisenhower stood on Portsdown Hill
Near Fort Southwick and looked out across at
The sunlit Solent, where ships assembled
Like a shoal of fish in a country stream,
Each moving and aware of its place in
The whole, which seemed to have one mind and will,
To join the force of five thousand boats that
Would shortly sail against cruel Hitler,
And felt the weight of his sole decision
That could preserve or wreck the fleet in storms.
Just as Achilles camped near the walls of
Troy and, smarting in his tent, eager for
Revenge, waited for Hector to appear
And planned the attack that would win the war,
So Montgomery camped in Southwick Park,
And, smarting from the defeat at Dunkirk,

And Rommel's escape at El Alamein,
Waited to engage him in Normandy
Like a hound for the fox to show his face.
Neither Eisenhower nor Montgomery
Knew they were being watched from higher worlds
By the twin forces of good and evil,
By intermediaries of bright Christ
And dark Satan. Tell, Muse, how this could be.

Tell, Muse, how the four-tiered cosmos became
The universe which is our home, how first
Primordial Nothingness, potential Fire
Was always everywhere, a moving power,
Empyrean of the infinite Whole,
Intelligence self-entangled, aware
As if an ocean were a mind of waves,
And knew "I am", the Kabbalah's Ayn Sof,
Transcendent darkness, latent beauty, God!
The all-knowing, wordless source of the Void,
Energy yearning for material form.
Infinite movement limited itself
Into a spiral, regular movement,
More dense, less dark than encompassing Whole
But as sea turns green in a sheltered bay
And its horizon remains indigo,
Though it divides within, it is still one,
So the spiralling darkness, the dark power
Iranians later called Ahriman
Who, independent, opposed the One Light,
Ahura, though sharing in creation,
Potential, latent Being, Void, Abyss,
Was one with its infinite subtle mind,
Which, by pressure, tension between the two,
As Nothingness pressed on this Non-Being,
Defined it more, thrust two pre-particles,
One of which took energy from its twin,
Annihilated it, became a point,
The singularity that Einstein saw,
The infinitesimal origin
Of Being, which through pressure from the Fire
(Moving Nothingness, spiralled Non-Being)
Expanded into thought, the demiurge
Iranians called Ahura Mazda,
Consciousness into which the Ayn Sof sent
A line of light across the dark Abyss,

Bright radiance of potential Existence,
Immanent universal energy
We know as Jehovah or the Logos,
In whose quantum vacuum manifest
In symmetry as in ordered pattern
The points – Kabbalists would say sephiroth –
Or seeds of pre-matter, pre-consciousness,
Spiritual archetypes, Ideas or Forms,
Emanations of forces without shapes,
Powers that became Lucifer, then Michael,
Gabriel and the angels, Adam Kadmon
(The first man) and the Cosmic Christ, the Light
Which transcendent Fire is when immanent;
And spawned evil as dark power pulled away
And rebel Lucifer became Satan,
Fallen adversary of the divine.
Being contained all opposites, yin-yang,
Contradictions, powers of Darkness and Light,
So "zero"'s Nothingness, Void-Plenitude,
Combined potentialities of all,
And through great pressure on Being squeezed out
Pairs of virtual particles, one of which
Attracted energy and became real
And survived in Existence as substance,
Form, structure, process, Becoming. Just as
A nut, warmed by sun, shoots into a tree,
So this nut within Fire branched into all
Leafy creation through a blaze. Its heat
Gave a hot beginning, several big bangs
Which squeezed ten millionths of a gram, compressed
New matter billions of times smaller than
A subatomic particle, and caused
A huge density that produced a force,
One superforce of scalar fields and then
Cosmic inflation into galaxies,
So that the tiny universe became
In one great whoosh the hugeness of all space
Which still expands, as Hubble has confirmed,
And which is held in place by Dark Matter
That has emerged from points like processes
Of atoms, consciousness, first living things,
And forms ninety-nine per cent of all mass.
As red sparks shoot upwards from a bonfire
Galaxies shot from the primordial Fire
And moved upwards and outwards in the dark

And glowed against the blackness of the Void;
A universe like dancing bonfire smuts,
Stars like fiery particles thrown off from
The burning substance of the latent Fire.
So there were now two forces, opposites,
Expanding Fire and contracting Darkness,
Antigravity and gravity held
In balance by a constant that controlled
The values of all atoms, yang and yin:
Creation that poured out of a white hole,
And destruction that swirled down a black hole.
And these two forces were embodied by
The Cosmic Christ and Satan, Light and Dark
Held in uneasy balance by wise God
Whose all-knowing prevents dualism,
A schism in the tension within Being.
And round one cooling smut of these sparks formed
An atmosphere of clouds round simmerings
Of molten lava, rocks and violent storms
And the right conditions for germs to swell,
Amoebae in waters, primeval sludge
Whence, mixing dark substance from stars and Light,
The first ancestors of mankind crawled out,
The aim and glory of this divine birth
And purpose in its manifestation,
To dwell in grass and trees with nuts and fruit
And live in peace with flora and fauna,
And ascend into self-organising
Hierarchical wholes through evolution.
Multiplicity pours out from the One,
Each second the Fire limits itself in
Some ten thousand million million million
Qualifications, modifications,
Events which co-exist in space or are
Ordered as sequences in time so that
Space and time are not real, but are derived
As co-existences or successions
Of events which have modified the Fire.
As hot sun on a sea raises moisture
Which forms a cloud and falls as drops of rain,
Our souls emerge from Being and take form,
Vital energy fills our limbed bodies,
Is captured by our brains as consciousness,
A universal force that gives us life
Until our souls take leave, evaporate,

Return like droplets to Being's great sea
Where all souls that have lived are gathered now
Like waves of shimmering sea round a rock
In brilliance of exploding, leaping light;
Or if their natures choose, like the dark waves
That wap restlessly on a moonless night.
Being contains both Paradise and Hell,
And who we are determines where we go.

Being is more bright, less dense than this world.
In landscapes of Being, closer to Light
The light is more intense and vital than
On earth, colours dazzle, which we absorb
In the transparent body that leaves flesh
Gladly when we discard our dense body,
And shows the Light that shines within to all.
At the level of Being, radiance,
Absolute Reality, divine sun
Which shines from the source as living spirit,
Is brighter than on earth and is received
As a bulb shines through a transparent glove
In a more subtle, responsive airness
Than our coarse physical body, which is
Like a leather glove that hides Light inside,
Which we put off on death, leaving within
The transparent soul-body radiant.
Soul, radiant, moves mind to a shorter
Frequency, faster vibrations, that can
Be taken for stillness, and differs from
Coarse thought as fine silk does from chicken wire.
Soul raises mind to its highest level.
Fine mind shone through by soul perceives all things
Within a unity; and still retains
Individuality as events
Mark each soul differently, like crayon marks
On the tubular glass of an oil-lamp.
And mind is not the rhythms of the brain,
But has a frequency too small to know.
Radiance is our true nature: the spirit
Shining into our soul with intense Light.
As bees swarm in a beehive and the young
Sip honey from the beeswax culled from flowers,
So souls in Heaven sip the honeyed Light.
In Heaven, souls between lives see from their
Airy, radiant, transparent soul-bodies

Gardens, trees, flowers, lush streams, clouds and rainbows
Whose reality, as if on a screen
When film shows waterfalls that are not there
When the projector stops, is but a dream.
So in beautiful gardens a white crowd
Gathered, all beings entitled to vote,
And, standing on a rock as above clouds,
Surrounded by Michael and Archangels
And thinkers like Augustine and artists
Who resembled stamens in a white rose,
Christ, the emanation who put on limbs
As the historical Zoroaster,
Lao-tzu, Krishna, Buddha, Jesus and then
Mohammed, embodying one message
Among all peoples in successive lives,
The Angel of the Lord in separate
Incarnations for each culture and creed
Which then became separate creations,
Limbs of the One, the Cosmic Christ from which
They materialised, independent
Souls in Heaven, like sons from one father
Only they were once *forms* of their father,
Avatars who descended with godhead
To earth in incarnate form from their source,
Incarnations *of* one emanation
On earth, and then in Heaven incarnations
From one emanation, separate souls;
Incarnate father on earth, sons in Heaven.
(So unity seeds multiplicity.)

His pure transparent body shining as
Does sunlight in crystal, too bright to see,
Christ spoke to the ring of radiance round him,
Which resembled petals of a white rose.
In English, the universal language,
He said in a tone urgent and serene:
"Souls of this Heaven, whose universal
Vision yearns to bring peace to the fallen earth,
And regards with disapproval what Satan
Is doing below, through his instrument
Hitler, whom he wishes to crown Kaiser
With charge of a terrible new weapon,
Know that the war has reached a crucial stage.
The Fascists seem to be winning; they hold
From Spain, the Habsburg seat, to Papal Rome

And what was the Holy Roman Empire
Which they revived under Satanic rule,
And in the Holy City, Nuremberg,
Have built a Coliseum, have begun
A stadium to seat half a million,
And a wide avenue where troops can march
When seven electors sit in the Castle
And proclaim Kaiser Adolf to the world.
They are preparing for their coming rule
Which will, they plan, include America,
The British Empire and USSR.
The Allies have assembled a great force,
The largest ever known, to invade France
But though they have retained surprise, a wall
Of concrete, Fortress Europe, awaits them
And success is not guaranteed. They have
One tenth of Germany's troops, and if they
Fall back into the sea as at Dunkirk
The war is over, Satan will have won.
Nothing is certain, mankind has freewill,
We don't know how the future will turn out,
Only God, the Fire, has total knowledge.
Souls of this Heaven, you who study know
That just as in this school of soul-making
The earth is a place where you test your souls
In limbs of temptation, you know the task
Of all on earth is to open to God,
Admit the Light we know, recover it
From the dark flesh in which the spark is trapped,
Open the prison gates so energy
From the divine will channels into men;
You know man co-creates the earth with God
Although most do not know the partnership,
That each pours his being into mankind,
Each grows his soul like grain, discards the stalk.
If Satan rules the earth, no Light will shine;
Darkness only, deception, illusion.
I, who lead your Coalition of souls,
Who represent the Light throughout the world,
The souls of every race and creed and kind,
Every region you lived in or will live
If you opt to return to help mankind –
As Cosmic Christ Pantokrator, who leads
The equivalent up here of a benign
Benevolent world government below –

I know you wish to help humanity,
To tilt the balance in favour of good
And keep our influence, despite freewill,
In the midst of universal evil.
Our scouts have lodged ideas in open minds;
But now we need to strengthen Eisenhower
Who is not as receptive as we wish.
We have to make the best of what we have,
Bearing in mind he was promoted through
Satan's agent of influence, Baruch.
We plant ideas in Montgomery's soul
When he opens in prayer at nine each night,
But we must redouble our efforts and
Pour strength into Eisenhower, our Caesar,
And screen his plan from Hitler and Rommel.
God, in whose Being we all live and move,
Wants this, though wordless, and has informed me
In infused wise guidance. Satan must not
Be allowed to rule unchallenged on earth.
I have now made the Archangel Michael
Responsible for the most successful
Outcome of Operation Overlord.
As above, below; as below, above.
As Land Commander-in-Chief he will now
Report to me, his Supreme Commander.
Please indicate that you approve this course
And that I have your full authority
To dispatch him on this urgent mission."
So spoke Christ; thousands of assembled souls
Concurred, expressed approval with a hum
As if a million bees, nuzzling at one
In a rose, fanned their wings with one accord,
And even as he spoke, there was movement
Round the edges as the newly arrived
Gathered, bewildered, from their battlefield.

At once Michael sped down towards the earth
Like a flash of lightning in energy
Once thought to be ether which fills space and
Connects Being to earth like morning mist.
Alighting on his Mount on the same rock
Off Marazion where fishermen saw
Him fifteen hundred centuries before,
He gathered the forces of wind and sea
Known as Boreas, Zephyrus, Neptune

Or Poseidon, and unleashed a great storm
Along the entire northern coast of France.
Round Calais rollers broke and crashed, huge waves
That could upturn and smash all landing craft.
Meanwhile a band of angels found Rommel
At La Roche Guyon and sent down the thought
That there would be no invasion until
The wind dropped, that he could visit his wife.
Other angels intercepted signals
To German intelligence and then warned
Of an attack in the Pas de Calais.

At Southwick House General Eisenhower
Listened, dismayed, in the conference of
The Allied Expeditionary Force
As Stagg, his weather-forecaster, announced:
"It will be overcast with Force Five winds,
Stormy." He asked Montgomery his view
As the Allied Land Forces Commander
Of Operation Overlord, who spoke:
"I have prepared the armies, it is now
For you as Supreme Commander to say
If the armies should go. The invasion
Fleet, five thousand ships, the biggest ever,
Is waiting, a decision to cancel
Must be announced twenty-four hours before
The landings." Air Chief Marshal Tedder spoke,
Eisenhower's deputy: "You can't invade
Through mountainous seas – look what happened to
The Spanish Armada – and with low cloud,
Which denies air cover." Smarting within,
Feeling the most senior in position,
A thought that Michael had lodged in his mind,
Montgomery spoke: "I am in favour
Of going. A huge operation has
Been co-ordinated, from Falmouth to
Dartmouth, Weymouth, Portsmouth and Newhaven
The soldiers are ready, morale is high,
We have surprise, the Germans are looking
At our phantom army around Dover,
If we don't go now, we must wait a month."
Frowning, Eisenhower spoke: "No decision
Will be made till tomorrow's conference,
The American Navy should now leave
Subject to last-minute cancellation."

The invasion fleet put out on rough sea
And Eisenhower was driven to his trailer
Which served as his office, hidden from all
In woods off Pitymoor Lane, where, safe from
Air raids, he sat, tense jaw thrust out, tense neck,
Which Kay, his Irish driver tried to ease
With kneading massage and a gentle kiss.
Only the Roman Julius Caesar
And the Norman William the Conqueror
Had successfully launched an invasion
Across the Channel, and his thoughts were deep
And with the storm-tossed men and their sickness
As they rolled on the swell.
A clear dawn broke
Over white-columned Southwick House. Stagg spoke:
"The cloud and wind are just five hours away."
Admiral Ramsay, Naval Commander-in-
Chief, AEF spoke: "I think we should go."
Air Chief Marshal Leigh-Mallory spoke, Air
Commander-in-Chief: "I am against, our
Air Forces could not carry out the plan."
Watching from Being, in the command post
Within the University of Souls,
As if on a live link-up on TV
By satellite, Michael beamed waves of power
Through the Fire to his opposite number
Below, Montgomery, who spoke: "Most of
The air programme can be done, we must go,
Each hour's delay makes the troops' ordeal worse.
We must invade from storm, and gain surprise."
Michael smiled approval. But then, gravely,
Eisenhower spoke: "Our ground forces are not
Overwhelmingly powerful, we need
Air cover or the landings are a risk,
And if air cover's lost in cloud, we must
Postpone. Any dissentient voices?"
Indignant but powerless to change his mind,
Michael beamed dissent at Montgomery,
Who, smarting at Tedder's being preferred,
Smouldered in silence, and preserved Allied
Unity of purpose and decision.
Eisenhower spoke: "D-Day is not June fifth."

As Eisenhower drove through green fields that day,
Down lanes to Broomfield House, the wind and rain

Swept through the scent of fresh-cut hay. He stopped
The car and gazed at a perfect rainbow,
An arc like a storm-god's bow, one end propped
By an oak-tree. Swallows skimmed low like planes.
He got out, stood and looked, ignoring Kay.
The hedgerows were alive. A tortoiseshell,
Wings spread, waited on a stinging nettle
To take off; a slug, snails, a cinnabar
Moth with vermilion hindwing, a toadstool,
And scarlet poppies splashed like blood across
The cornfield. All Nature glistened and thrust,
Burgeoning with life in the still and peace
Of the deep English countryside, where war
Had scarcely reached. The grass stirred at his feet,
A hedgehog crawled like a cumbersome tank,
Oblivious of the storm of war which he,
Like an angry god, was about to roll
Like thunder. Eisenhower's eyes filled with tears.

Eisenhower dined at Broomfield House alone
With Montgomery, rain lashing the glass,
And the brave-hearted beret-wearer spoke:
"If we don't go on the sixth, we can't till
The nineteenth, and to stand men down and bring
Back ships will damage their morale and lose
Them their surprise. We have to make it work."
The Supreme Commander spoke: "You are right.
If we have air superiority,
We have to go." They drove through wind and rain
To white-columned Southwick House. Eisenhower
Sat at a table in the mess room, while
The other SHAEF commanders poured coffee
And sat in easy chairs. Stagg spoke: "We saw
A break in the weather this afternoon.
We now agree, the depression will slow
Down in mid-Atlantic. The rain will stop
In two or three hours, there will be quiet seas
And little cloud for perhaps a day on
June the sixth." Suddenly all cheered, and then
Rear Admiral Creasy, Ramsay's Chief of Staff,
Eagerly, and, gravely, Air Chief Marshal
Leigh-Mallory cross-examined Stagg with
Major-General de Guingand. Ramsay smiled.
Leigh-Mallory and Tedder were anxious
About the effectiveness of heavy

Bombers. Ramsay spoke: "If Overlord is
To happen on June the sixth as I hope,
The American task force Commander
Must be told in the next half hour. The next
Time the tides are right is June the nineteenth."
Eisenhower pondered in isolation.
Bedell Smith, his loyal Chief of Staff, spoke:
"It's a helluva gamble, but it is
The best gamble." Montgomery was asked
And spoke: "I would say: Go." Eisenhower asked:
"What are the air ramifications of
A decision to go?" And having heard,
Urged on by Michael's thought-power, he said:
"I am quite positive that the order
Must be given for the convoys to put
To sea. A final irrevocable
Decision will be made at four-thirty."
They left the mess. Kay drove bold Eisenhower
To his trailer. The wind blew violently,
Rain lashed in lines as if a hurricane
Whirled through the woods and whined among the trees
Like a storm that would stop a fleet, not act
As cover. Eisenhower paced up and down
Between the ashtrays filled with smouldering
Cigarettes, blood pressure up, headache, gas
Pains in his stomach. Hands on hips, he stared
At the drizzling dark, and drank pot after
Pot of coffee, and smoked and listened as
The rain dripped on the roof of the trailer
From overhanging trees like the ticking
Of a grandfather clock.

At four-thirty
In Southwick House, Stagg told the commanders:
"The rain will clear within a matter of
Hours." Eisenhower, pacing, shot out his chin
Like a tortoise, no longer prone to hide
Under his armoured shell but ready to
Begin a plodding advance with great stealth,
And asked, "Who's for go?" Admiral Ramsay spoke:
"Spotting for naval gunfire concerns me,
But I will take the risk." Tedder said, "I
Am ready." Leigh-Mallory spoke thus: "Air
Conditions are below the minimum."
Stagg left, and brave Eisenhower pensively

Spoke: "The ships are sailing in the Channel.
If they must be called back, it must be now.
The Supreme Commander alone can do
That." He stopped and thought, and all power was his.
All round the earth the atmosphere trembled,
Awaiting the disturbance of his words
As an ocean awaits a whipping wind.
Eisenhower spoke: "OK, let's go." A cheer
Went up, and everyone rushed from the mess
To their command posts. Eisenhower was left
Sitting in lonely isolation. Now
It was too late to change the decision.
Not even he could stop the invasion.

Orders went to ships already at sea
Or in crowded harbours, to commanding
Generals and Allied statesmen. Churchill came
To the trailer, de Gaulle, Smuts and others.
Messages were received from Washington,
From London and Montgomery. At six
Eisenhower stopped the frantic to-and-fro.
With Kay driving, his dutiful chauffeur,
He visited three airfields near Newbury,
Drove up, got out and walked among the men,
And when they realised who he was word passed
Like a wind blowing across a meadow
And a great roar went up and all shouted
"Good old Ike!" and cheered and whistled, thumbs up.
He spoke to tense troops with blackened faces.
Morale was high, the banter quick as he
Shook each warmly by the hand, looked each one
In the eye and wished him success – "Good luck" –
And reassured each, putting each at ease,
Aware that he might be sending each man
To a machine-gunned death before daybreak,
And smiled broadly at each "General, we'll take
Care of Rommel for you, don't you worry".
Then he climbed to the HQ building's roof,
And waves of planes roared into the sunset,
Some towing gliders filled with fighting men,
And soon it had grown dark and a full moon,
So brilliant it cast shadows, lit the sky
Where hundreds of planes circled overhead
Like a dark flock of migrating swallows
That swarm and soar and eddy in the air

Till all latecomers have joined and they can
Set off together south for warmer climes.
From time to time they blotted out the moon.
Eisenhower, standing with his head held back,
Hands in his pockets, face tipped to the sky,
Watched them go with tears in his eyes, and said:
"Hundred and First Airborne. Eighty per cent
Casualties L-M reckons. It's on."
Kay in uniform and cap ached for him,
Seeing he wore responsibility
Like a star actor's smiling performance
Whose current leaves him drained and tearful in
The dressing-room when the curtain is down.
Her body yearned, but she saluted him
And looked away from his wet eyes as he
Walked slowly with bent head, and said, "It's on,
No one can stop it now," stooped and sat in
The back of his staff car, and was silent
As they drove back along the moonlit road
To the trailer in the woods at Southwick.

Eisenhower sat in his trailer, in his
Advance headquarters hidden in thick woods
Which he used as an office, and waited
For the first reports. Hours passed. Overhead
The roar and drone of planes rising, heading
Across the Channel, waves of bombers that
Would shield the men landing on the beaches.
His eyes were bloodshot, his hand shook each time
He lit a cigarette and waited, tense.
He could have sat with Churchill and de Gaulle,
With fifty commanders in Southwick House
Or nearby Portsmouth, but he now preferred
Solitude in his trailer, shared with Kay
Who every so often stood behind him
And massaged his shoulders, but though he said
"Um, that's good" she could not undo the knots
At the base of his neck and relax him.
And as she watched his torture, his waiting
For the outcome of gambling with the lives
Of hundreds of thousands of men, all quiet
Save for the roaring of each wave of planes,
She thought of how he flew from Washington
To Scotland and came down by train into
A January fog six months before,

And how she drove him to a large town house
Off Berkeley Square and they had a nightcap
And he gave her a portrait of Roosevelt
Signed by the President to her, and then,
Alone, how they were in each other's arms,
How ties came off and jackets, how buttons were
Unbuttoned, and then how, his face snuggled
In the hollow of her neck and shoulder,
He said "Oh God, Kay, I'm sorry I am
Not going to be any good for you";
And how, a man of fifty-three, he was
Exhausted by his flight and train journey
And two weeks' briefings at the Pentagon;
How he said "I told you that I was out
Of practice in love" and she said "I should
Have known how exhausted you were. I know
That some day we're going to"; and how he
Had said they'd move to Telegraph Cottage
Near Bushey Park. But, massaging his neck,
She reflected that despite their move there
(With Butcher, Mickey, Moaney, Hunt and Smith)
The nearest they had come was one morning,
Sitting by the fire in the sun, when he
Had talked about his wife Mamie, the hurt
They had both felt when their older son died
Of scarlet fever, caught from a young maid,
So deep that they could not recapture love
Although they had tried. In halting, low words
He said: "I'm not the lover you should have,
It killed something in me, not all at once.
For years I never thought of making love.
Activity helps. And then when I did,
When it had been on my mind for weeks I
Failed, I failed with you, my dearest." Red-eyed
He muttered, "Somehow I just lost the way."
And then, his appointments secretary,
She booked his meetings, took his telephone
Calls, showed visitors into his office.
And now, with planes roaring for Normandy
And his neck still rigid with tension knots,
Would not be the time when he would relax.
Overflowing with love, she waited with
Him till at four she said, "I think you ought
To go and lie down for a little while."
And they went back to quarters, to the tent

Near Southwick House where, in an Indian
Village, he had spent hours sitting alone,
Checking every calculation from all
Points of view, American, English, French,
Canadian, Czech, Polish; the only man
Who had all phases of the plan in mind.
There he lay down but still sleep would not come.
He lay like a tired sailor on shore leave
Who feels the ground still roll like a ship's deck.

Like a long cord with knots, after Dieppe,
Built at the command of mighty Hitler,
From Norway to the Spanish border stretched,
All along the coast, a wall of concrete,
Fortress Europe. The coastal batteries
Of the Atlantic Wall, some a foot thick,
Controlled the coastline, while the batteries
On the German Navy dominated
Coastal shipping. The Atlantic Wall ran
From Norway and Denmark to Germany,
The Netherlands, Belgium and France, thick round
The Pas de Calais (ninety-three gun sites),
Normandy (twenty-seven), the Channel Isles,
And round the west to Bordeaux and Biscay.
Huge deep-dug bunkers frowned with heavy guns,
Artillery, machine-gun emplacements,
Anti-aircraft guns, fire-direction towers.
Even the gentle sea hid hostile things,
Mined posts and steel hedgehogs under water;
Steel girders eighteen feet below low tide
To rip open or obstruct landing craft;
The beaches bristled with tank obstacles
Like dragons' teeth, and beyond the ramped wall
Of sand dunes were land mines and anti-tank
Ditches, coastal defence guns and shelters
Adorned with rolled barbed wire. Western Europe
Had a shield of concrete which Rommel now
Inspected and improved, adding more steel
And four million more mines in belts that were
From one to eight thousand yards wide. New beach
Defences, thick pillboxes and strongpoints
At the water's edge and wide belts of mines
(Rommel's asparagus, mines set on poles)
Were formidable obstacles that were
Covered by fire, all manned by ruthless men.

Inland, the Maginot Line guarded French
Borders with Luxembourg and Germany
With machine-gun turrets and slit bunkers,
While the West Wall on Germany's borders
With the Netherlands, Belgium, Luxembourg
And France comprised miles of rows of concrete
Anti-tank obstacles shaped like sand-pies,
And armour-plated bunkers and turrets.
Behind great walls Germany felt secure.
With Rommel away from La Roche Guyon
Speidel drank till one, then prepared to sleep.

The airborne assault came out of the night
In silence and stealth, like three noiseless owls.
British Sixth Airborne paratroops were first.
Midnight, and three gliders cast off from their
Tug aircraft and silently, using maps
And stop-watches, the pilots descended
Five thousand feet of pitch darkness, and then,
Like owls with outstretched wings, looking for mice,
Skimming the fields, smashed into the barbed wire
Defences round Bénouville's two bridges.
The crew of the first glider were knocked out,
The second glider landed fifteen yards
Away, the third in a marshy pond, where
One man was drowned. Regaining consciousness,
Howard's men burst from the first glider, and
Charged and captured Pegasus Bridge to hold
It so no German reinforcements met
The seaborne landings on the beaches. More
Paratroops dropped from the moonlit sky like
A flurry of snowflakes drifting down, and
Destroyed five bridges across the Dives
Whence William the Conqueror sailed, and more
Landed near Ouistreham across the Orne
And destroyed Merville's coastal battery
Which could have shelled the assault on Sword beach.

The American airborne drop followed.
At one-thirty, laden with heavy loads,
Out of the night waves of American
Paratroops, Screaming Eagles, Hundred and
First Airborne, dropped into marshes, some far
From the northern exits from Utah beach
Like dislodged autumn leaves whirled in a wind.

Some areas were flooded and some men drowned.
The French Resistance spread confusion, false
(Dummy) drops, alerted by messages
In code on radio. Two groups of men
From 506th fell on Ste Mère-Eglise
And were killed by Germans; Eighty-second
Airborne dropped near, some fell in the centre,
One hung from the church tower as battle raged
Like a spider in a gossamer web
That has been broken by a wilful boy
And played dead while his comrades died below.
More fell into the swamp of Meredet.
By five Ste Mère-Eglise was well secure.

Seventy-four of ninety-two radar
Stations on the Normandy coast had been
Bombed, a fake naval armada was towed
Towards the Pas de Calais. Misinformed,
The German attention was on Calais.
General Marcks received reports of air drops
In the Orne estuary and Cotentin
Peninsula, and notified Pemsel
Who told Speidel, Rommel's Chief of Staff, who
Informed Rundstedt, who wished to order up
Two more tank divisions. Rundstedt cabled
Hitler in his Obersalzberg Berghof,
Near the mountain town of Berchtesgaden.
Michael hovered. It was late, and looking
At Calais, and confused by Fortitude,
Hitler refused to send the tanks and took
A sleeping draught and went to bed and slept
Like a tired sentry who expects a shout,
As did Rommel in Herrlingen. In Caen
The 21st Panzers were ready at
Two a.m., but no one gave the order.

Hitler, whether at the Berghof as now
Or his Wolf's Lair in Prussian Rastenburg,
Controlled the war on eastern and western
Fronts, and trusting maps and his own instincts,
Ignored his Generals. Keitel head of
The OKW did not oppose
Him, and, lacking air or sea power (which were
Under Göring, Himmler, Dönitz), Rundstedt,
Commander-in-Chief for the Western Front,

Kept quiet when Hitler focused on the east
And ignored the west, US and sea power.
Rommel commanded Army Group B and
Defended France and Belgium and the coasts
Under Rundstedt, who thought the Atlantic
Wall could not hold up an invasion more
Than a day, and that the Panzer Group West
Divisions should be held inland. His plan
Was to give ground in Normandy and keep
Reserves intact. Rommel wanted his tanks
Forward to stop landings, not back to face
Fighter-bombers; two armoured divisions
Near Calais and more held back by Rundstedt
Could not be moved without Hitler's orders.
Only 21st Panzers were near Caen.

The greatest invasion fleet ever sent,
Five thousand ships, bobbed in the still dark waves
Off the fortified coast of Normandy.
From the shore it resembled a distant
Flock of dark sea-birds caught in the storm and
Riding out danger on the choppy sea.
The American air attack began
At three as five hundred tons of bombs rained
Down on each of the largest coastal gun
Batteries round the Vire, whose estuary
Separated Utah and Omaha
Beaches, and into which troops had to thrust
To join the two beachheads. As it grew light,
The big ships of the Western Task Force, watched
By General Bradley from the *Augusta*,
Opened up with their guns, battered the shore.
To be out of range of the German guns
The Americans transferred to assault
Craft much further out than the British. Each
Large infantry transport trailed a barrage
Balloon to deter low German aircraft
As the troops climbed down into assault craft,
And sat squashed between two high ends. Some grinned,
Some were lost in thought near the choppy sea.
Soon many were seasick as for three hours
They surged forward, forty helmeted men
Crouching, laden as waves smashed round their sides,
Cold, drenched, and watching as craft swamped and sank.
A naval and air bombardment lasted

Forty-five minutes, towards six-thirty
The assault craft came in an hour after
Low water and in front of the German
Beach defences, which would be covered by
The sea at high tide, and the large, heavy
German guns thus had nothing to shoot at.
Despite the bombardment of the shoreline
Salvos of German shells plumed up with spray.
Michael watched anxiously as they headed
Towards the most defended Utah beach,
And ordered Neptune to make great tidal
Currents, which pushed the assault craft on to
The Grand Dune marshes two thousand yards south.
Here the first troops landed without loss, led
By President Theodore Roosevelt's son,
And nearly thirty Sherman tanks, and now
All assault craft turned south to this new beach
While for three hours German artillery
Fired blindly at a beach devoid of men.
The troops pressed inland through the marshes and
Linked up with Hundred and First paratroops.

D-Day, day of decision, departure,
Disembarkation or defeat, D for
The Day (en Français J-Jour) and H for
The Hour, which fluctuated on the coast
Like high tide. Half light, the tossing sea was
Filled with assault craft. Sea-sprayed, men hunched in
Helmets and packs, rose and fell, surged forward.
Hearts in mouths, none spoke. All looked at the beach,
A distant line of sand, holding rifles,
Moving forward stealthily as a fox
Approaches a farmyard, creeping at night.
Who would be dead in a few minutes as
H-hour approached? What hand to hand combat?
The infantry went in, silent heroes.
Splash! Down went the flap into a ramp. Choke
With admiration and awe as each stood
Up and jumped into three feet of water,
Rifle held up, the cold chill of the sea
Shuddering through, and waded forward as
Machine-guns chattered like awakened geese
That honked indignantly in the silence.

Omaha beach, a long bluff and a height,

A hundred and seventy feet, above
A strip of shingle vehicles could not cross
And five defended exits through the cliff,
An infantry division well dug in.
Bad weather and great surf. Aircraft bombed blind
And missed, naval gunners saw few targets,
Sherman tanks and guns launched over three miles
Out sank, as did ten infantry assault
Craft, while more had their bottoms ripped out by
Rommel's underwater obstacles, and
Laden infantrymen drowned. Currents pushed
Some troops ashore two miles off their target
On defended beaches; without tanks or
Engineers they were pinned down, equipment
Lost in the surf, units mixed up. Some troops
Crouched in their craft under a hail of fire,
Fear in their stomachs as each bullet whipped
Up the rough sea beside them, and then bang!
Down went the flap – the ramp – and they stood up,
A Hell of smoke ahead from the shelling,
And jumped into three feet of cold water
And waded past corpses of their comrades,
The sea dark with blood in crimson patches,
And staggered, wet, onto the sand and – "Mines" –
Followed a path through, ducking constant fire,
Under the cliffs of the bluff which rang out,
And huddled under what little cover
They could find, unable to leave the beach,
As crabs left high and dry by an ebb-tide
Crouch under stones or burrow into sand.
Two or three thousand were wounded, or killed.
At nine on *Augusta*, Bradley prepared
To abandon Omaha. Destroyers,
Steaming in close, shelled pillboxes, and then
General Cota stood and with his pistol
Waved forward the 29th Division,
Walking upright amid the German fire,
And General Canham shouted to 16th
Infantry, "They are murdering us here,
Let us move inland and get murdered there."
Gathering round brave leaders such as these,
The troops began to fight through German blocks
Up the draws and then off the beach, and by
Midday they were on top of the long bluff
And heading for Coleville a mile inland

To take the eighteen mile long stretch between
Isigny on the Vire and near Bayeux.

At Pointe du Hoc thee miles west of that beach
A German battery of six guns thumped
On a sheer cliff a hundred feet above
A stretch of beach just twenty-five yards wide.
Their range covered all the Omaha beach,
No bombing or shelling had silenced them.
More than two hundred Rangers trained in cliff
Assaults, with rope grapnels and extension
Ladders, drifted eastwards on the current
And landed on the cratered beach, which would
Not take their equipment. Through savage fire,
The Rangers fitted metal tube sections
Into long ladders and, firing ropes, climbed
The steep cliff towards guns, hanging, rising
Like spiders on silk threads. As the Germans
Fell back, they found the casemates empty, for
The guns were camouflaged further inland.
These the Rangers destroyed at close quarters.

The main British aerial bombardment
Of the Atlantic Wall and the inland
Defences began at three, before first
Light, with puffs of smoke like distant campers'
Fires, and British and Canadian troops
Transferred to assault craft seven miles out
And came in at seven-thirty, an hour
Later than the Americans, giving
More time to silence guns. The craft nosed in
At five one-mile zones of a twenty-four
Miles long beach, bringing crouching, helmeted
Men to Gold beach, whose target was Bayeux
And then to link with the American
Troops off Omaha at Port en Bessin;
And men to Sword beach, their task to take Caen;
And Canadians to Juno, to take
The road between Bayeux and Caen, and link
Up with the British. At Gold many guns
Were out of action as the assault craft
Beached at high tide and in a force five wind,
And the men jumped down and ran up the slope
To the sand dunes and farmland beyond it.
To the west, from Arromanches rocks lay off

The shore; a cliff rose which further along
Became the Omaha bluff, and Germans
Dug in, enfiladed and raked the bay.
Amphibious tanks designed by Hobart
Helped the troops overcome German strongpoints
And press inland. Others passed Le Hemel
And La Rivière, and Stanley Hollis
Of the Sixth Green Howards cleared a German
Pillbox and captured twenty-five prisoners
And won the only Victoria Cross
To be awarded on D-Day. As troops
Pressed forward, more, landing, took their places,
Including the Desert Rats. At Sword beach
Some seasick men came in near Ouistreham
Hearing officers read through megaphones
Henry the Fifth's "Once more unto the breach".
The beach was congested, the infantry
Moved off without support from tanks; minutes
Later came Commandos with Lord Lovat,
Who stepped ashore with his piper, who played
His bagpipes up the sand to lift morale.
Just as the Etruscans were amazed when
Horatius held the Sublician bridge
Alone till the Romans had cut it down,
So stunned were the defenders when they saw
A kilted Scot walk unarmed up the beach
Playing bagpipes as if on a loch's slopes
And, astonished, no sniper thought to shoot,
A tale that will be told three thousand years.
Lovat reached Pegasus Bridge two minutes
Late and apologised for the delay
To the tired paratroops who still held it.
La Brèche and Ouistreham both fell, and bad
Weather and the rising tide now reduced
Sword beach to fifteen yards of sand, drowning
Wounded soldiers who could not move, and tanks
Landed behind schedule and then queued in
Traffic jams, and the British timetable
Fell behind. The infantry met tanks of
21st Panzers three miles from Caen, and
Though they summoned armour they were too late
To take Caen that day. More Panzers attacked
Towards Sword beach, their commander was told,
"If you don't push the British back into
The sea, we will have lost the war." These tanks

Rolled down and were stopped just short of the cliffs.
The Panzers had lost nearly half their tanks,
And though they had not thrust the invasion
Back into the sea, the British had been
Stopped before Caen just as scurrying ants,
Carrying minute specks, stop at a stone
That blocks their way, and return to their nest.

On Juno beach the Canadians (some
Of whom were French and were fighting for France),
A few minutes later than the British,
Landed in worsening weather and rough
Seas without tank support, the German land
Defences intact. The first men who jumped
From the assault craft were shot, the surf broke
Over corpses. A landing craft was hit
And sank, its men lost their weapons and came
Ashore with knives. But otherwise it was
The most successful D-Day landing, and
Though the beach narrowed with the rising tide
And traffic jams slowed down armoured support,
The infantry advanced through the minefields
Of the Atlantic Wall and linked up with
The Gold British at Creully and then reached
Their objective of the Bayeux-Caen road.

Eisenhower (and above, Michael) reviewed
The progress of the Allies on all fronts,
Poring over his map's flagged positions.
He had hoped for one beachhead sixty miles
Long and ten miles inland, with pressure on
Villers-Bocage and Falaise, but on all
Five beaches goals and link-ups were behind.
However, the Allies were ashore and
Through the Atlantic Wall everywhere but
At Omaha, and the Germans had failed
To stop the landings, and two divisions
Had been destroyed, two mauled, while the Allies
Had lost five thousand men. There had been no
Bloodbath. Eisenhower had achieved his aim.
The battle for Normandy had begun.

Back for the fiftieth anniversary,
Stand in the neat British cemetery at
Bénouville or Bayeux, white slabs on well

Looked after mown turf, flowers peeping through.
And at Pointe du Hoc, among shell craters
(Now grassed over) and broken blockhouses
With slits, look down the cliffs to the shale beach
Where two hundred and twenty-five Rangers
Stormed up with grappling ropes; only ninety
Survived. Look left and right from this great height
To uninterrupted cliff, as far as
The eye can see, reflect how many men
Were butchered here and now lie under white
Crosses in the vast cemetery. And how
At twelve-thirty that fateful morn, battered,
The Americans were set to withdraw
Back to the sea but for volunteers who
Pushed themselves forward in waves and carried
The day for freedom, sun-spoked Liberty.
Go to the cemetery on Omaha
Cliffs, see nine thousand white crosses in ranks,
Straight and diagonal whichever way,
And see the cliffs over the yellow sand,
Reflect that the crack German division
Gave them no chance – no cover here – and stand
By the huge victory of a leaping boy
And look at arrows where the armies thrust,
Then walk through the rose-garden, red roses
Under a host of names, smell pines nearby,
See the scaffolded television tower.
Here the President will stand on the plinth.
And as we await a New World Order,
Look back on D-Day after fifty years.

At Herrlingen, Rommel, in dressing-gown,
Was arranging his wife's birthday presents
In the quiet drawing-room at six-thirty
When the phone rang and Speidel told him of
The airborne landings near the Norman coast,
And said, "It is not yet clear whether this
Is the long-expected invasion." At
Ten Rommel rang and Speidel said: "It is
The real thing, assault from air and sea."
Rommel stared, knowing the war was now lost
As the enemy were off the beaches,
And the professional soldier vied with
The patriot who would save Germany
From destruction by the Western powers,

And who saw that the obstacle to peace
Was the man in whose genius he believed,
The dictator who, if he won, would be
The greatest man in history, ruler
Of more territory than anyone
Had held: Alexander, Napoleon.

At the Berghof on the Obersalzberg,
Wooded slopes above, green prospect towards
Berchtesgaden and distant mountain range,
The Untersberg where Charlemagne still slept
And would arise to restore the glory
Of the medieval German Empire,
Hitler slept. His military adjutants
Conferred about the invasion, knowing
He would say, "It is a feigned attack to
Draw our troops from the real invasion site,"
Not wanting to be accused of judging
The situation wrongly. Jodl said,
"Nothing can be done till daybreak," and so
They let him sleep, and wake, and take breakfast,
And then, in the salon, in conference
Round the round table in comfortable chairs,
Hesitant, apologetic, as if
Conveying cables they did not believe,
Wary as mice of a golden eagle,
They told him. He was calm, and scoffed at "these
Confusing reports": "Our intelligence
Services are incompetent, agents
Paid by the Allies have planted this news
To lure me into sending divisions
Too soon and to the wrong place – a decoy!
We must throw the Allies into the sea.
I won't pass this to Paris, it would make
Our staffs nervous." Then he became angry:
"Again and again I warned Rommel and
Rundstedt, the first invasion will come in
Normandy. In March I warned the Generals
Several times. On May the sixth I phoned
Jodl that I attached particular
Importance to Normandy. But Rommel
And Rundstedt were convinced the invasion
Would take place in the Straits of Dover. Now
The enemy is where we can attack
Them." And then, turning to Bormann: "I am

Not worried. I do not believe that this
'Invasion' is more than a diversion.
I have always said that the main attack
Will come in the Pas de Calais where our
Atlantic Wall will cause a new Dunkirk."
Addressing all his Generals, he said:
"The Allies cannot deflect us from our
Purpose, a German Jew-free world empire.
I speak as Will, we are invincible.
I will pay Britain back with reprisal
Weapons, Vergeltungswaffe ones, V-1s,
Reprisal weapon ones. Know that I have
Eight thousand rocket-driven flying bombs,
Each with a one-ton warhead, pilotless
With a jet engine. Prepare to send the
First of these to London. I will attack
London. I will rain destruction. Our tests
On the atomic bomb have reached a new
Experimental stage. Soon, with a bomb
No larger than a pineapple, I will
Reduce a four kilometre zone in
Central London to a waste of rubble,
No one alive."
At noon he considered
The request by Field Marshal von Rundstedt,
Commander-in-Chief, West, that the Panzer
Reserves should be sent against the beachhead.
At two-thirty the order was given.
It was then too late to arrive that day,
And enemy bombing delayed them till
Daylight had probed the sky like a searchlight.

Satan soon learned of the sea-invasion.
Satan cannot read human thoughts, but can
Watch our countenances or our auras,
Which display the feelings of our stirred souls.
Demons, his spies, are just as deductive
Michael had enclosed a square area
From south England to central Normandy
In a wall of protective Light, the same
Invisible shield that is round Heaven.
Demons, flying like moths or beetles in
The night, were stopped as if by window glass,
And so saw nothing of Eisenhower's fleet.
Outside the shield, Being bobbed like the sea.

Like sun-flecks on a vast and moving tide
Spirits, both good and evil, hover near
Human beings, select a pair and dance,
Urging a man and woman to make love,
Future parents, so they are born on earth.
In the spirit world they have bonded, out
Of the love they have known forever, with
Spirit brothers and sisters, who agree
To come to earth as family or friends
And work together to improve the earth.
All is a great pattern as on a loom.
Spirits in their bodies a short time know
Their deaths were appointed before their births
And help the parents grow, that all is done
For the growth of the spirits of others –
Abortions, handicapped children, childhood
Fatalities, or death in war. We come
To earth, like choosing a course in a school,
At different levels of spiritual
Development, are born in the stations
That suit our spiritual needs, our love
And light. Sometimes we sacrifice our time
On earth for a spirit we've bonded with,
And helping others is a virtue, and
Coming to earth for a time furthers our
Spiritual growth. So was it with all those
Whose lives were cut short by the reaper's scythe
On D-Day. So hovered Arch-Satan's spies,
Buffeting again and again the shield
Of Light. And flitting round south-east England,
Some demons realised that something was wrong
And hastened back to Hell to tell Satan.

Tell, Muse, how Hell differs from Heaven, how
Heaven and Hell are places, regions in
The spirit world where like states of soul go –
Those ruled by positive or negative
Energy, by light or dark. Souls are drawn
To one region or the other by what
They have achieved and shaped: those filled with light,
Love, goodness, kindness, patience, charity,
Their thoughts controlled by calm for soul rules mind,
Hope; and those filled with darkness, hatred, fear
(Which Satan uses), unkindness, despair,
Intolerance, selfishness, envy and

Discouragement. Our desires run our souls,
Our thoughts have power, our souls know where to go
As when a man enters a crowded room
And, seeing strangers and familiar smiles,
Is drawn to those he knows and stands with them.
So our souls go to Heaven, or to Hell.
Heaven, the universal energy,
Positive power of God, Angels, sub-gods,
Spiritual beings, the saved, is known as
Yahweh's abode, where followers of Christ
Go; as Moslem joy and bliss; as Chinese
Divine will which guards the moral laws of
Man and the physical laws of nature;
As Mahayana home for enlightened
Ones; as Theravada extinction of
Desires; as home of Hindu Vishnu's Light
In Swarga, the domain of the devas.
To here are drawn all whose souls are white light
For bright light merges with bright light as do
Two lamps in a room, and a lit soul comes
Here of its own volition, drawn by Light
To the highest of seven levels of
Reducing brightness, the lowest being
An outer greyness for mere church-goers.
Hell, the universal energy or
Negative power of Satan, the abode
Or state of being of evil spirits
Or dark souls in an underworld, is known
As a gloomy island (Hades); abyss
(Tartarus); a dark region where shades thirst
(Sheol); a cold, dark place (Niflheimr, or
Hel); celestial clouds (Pueblo Indians);
A freezing and ill-smelling place (Iran);
An infernal reign of dread punishment
(Gehenna); a crater of fire beneath
A narrow bridge (Islamic Jahannam);
Twenty-one regions in the netherworld
(Hindu); a torture-chamber (Jain bhumis);
Multiple regions for different bodies
(Buddhist); a place of punishment (Chinese);
And a place of eternal damnation
For unrepentant sinners, the fiery
Domain of the Devil and his evil
Angels, separation from the good in
A fiery after-life. Hell is in fact

A dark region of gloomy fetid caves
In the nether spirit world, hung above
A bottomless abyss, and near a fire.
To here are drawn those whose souls are shadows,
For dark shadow is drawn to dark shadow,
Shuns the bright light which is painful to it,
And the darkest souls are willingly drawn
To the lowest of seven levels of
Reducing darkness, the highest being
An outer greyness for mere church-goers.

Tell, Muse, how demons differ from Angels.
Heaven and Hell have Angels and demons,
Departed spirits, each with counterpart.
Just as in fields of light under the Christ
Nine orders of higher and low Angels,
Peopling positive energy that beams
From the higher spirit world into form,
Occupy seven circles of great joy,
So in the caverns of the underworld
Under the Prince of Darkness, nine orders
Of loathsome demons hostile to mankind,
Peopling negative energy that swirls
From the lower spirit world into shape,
Occupy seven circles of grim dark.
Like Hindu avatars, curved asparas,
And Buddhist bodhisattvas Angels are
Supernatural beings who act as
Messengers from the Supreme Being, as
Intermediaries between Heaven
And earth, for God who created all things,
Set pure spirits with intellect and will
To watch over and cherish his creatures.
Some are Angels of punishment, Angels
Of death visit the dying, protective
Angels watch over all mortals, Angels
Of intercession carry prayers to God.
There are Angels of light and darkness, of
Destruction and holiness. In each faith
Angels of nations guard religious Truth.
The Mesopotamians knew Nebo,
The Angel of the Lord, and messengers
Called Sukalli, intermediaries.
Zoroastrians knew seven Angels:
Spenta Mainyu, Vohu Manah, Asha,

Armaiti, Khshathra Vairya, Haurvatat
And Ameretat. Judaism knew
Seven bright Archangels: Michael, who was
Commander-in-Chief of the angelic hosts,
Guardian of Israel and Christian Europe,
Ruler of Chaos; Uriel, leader
Of the heavenly hosts, guardian of Sheol,
The underworld; Raphael, healer of all
Human spirits; Gabriel, ruler of
Paradise, Cherubim and Seraphim;
Raguel, avenger of God; Sariel
Or Saqraquel, avenger of spirits;
And Remiel, guardian of souls in Sheol.
Phanuel fended off the evil Satans.
Other Angels are Zaphkiel, Angel of
Contemplation; Sandalphon, guardian;
And the Sophia, goddess of wisdom
Known to Gnostics and Orthodox Christians.
Christian Angels are in a hierarchy,
A choir of higher and lower Angels:
Angels, Archangels, Virtues and Powers,
Principalities, Dominions and Thrones,
Cherubim and fiery Seraphim
Who fly like hawks, each fluttering six wings,
And, highest of all Angels, Metatron
(Formerly the well-known prophet Enoch).
Four-faced Cherubim bore Yahweh's great throne,
Seraphim influenced mortals with God's love,
Ophanim, Thrones, were fiery wheels, each with
A ring of eyes, mounts of the Cherubim.
Arab Islamic Angels include four
Throne-bearers of Allah, Cherubim who
Praise Allah, four Archangels – Jibril, the
Revealer; Mikal, the great provider;
Izrail, the dreadful Angel of Death; and
Israfil, Angel of the Last Judgement.
Gnostics knew Aeons and Archons, there are
Manichaean Angels. Angels may take
Many forms simultaneously, but
Are mostly light-shapes in great radiance,
Like flecks of dust in a summer sun-shaft.
The Babylonians and Assyrians and
Early Hebrews knew non-human evil
Spirits. The Sumerian utukku,
Alu (demons), lilu (ghosts) and gallu

(Bull-devils) include rabisu (lurkers)
And the female labartu, labasu
And ahazzu (seizers), the male Lilu,
Female Lilitu (Lilith) and Ardat
Lili, plague-demon Namtar, Ashakku,
Demon of fevers and disease. Their world
Was full of harmful spirits (mazzikin)
Which swarm in house and field and lower air.
The demons of the Old Testament are
Flying fiery serpents and scorpions,
Hairy goat-form se'irim, beast-like satyrs,
Wolves, jackals, the wild creature Azazel,
Lilith, the night demon (of the triad
Known in Babylon and Assyria);
Deber (pestilence) and Keteb (noonday
Destruction), and vampire-like Alukah;
And Shedim, winged bulls who guard temples.
The Arab demons, jinn, were everywhere
Though not perceptible by our senses,
The most dangerous being the ghul (ghoul),
A female who lay in wait and enticed
A man at night and carried him away.
Demons buzz, hum or whistle in deserts,
And Arabs called trailing serpents "shaitan".
The Iranians knew many demons.
The demons created by Ahriman
Are innumerable Drujes, Dryvants,
Pairikas and Dragons, who spread deceit
From evil will throughout the seven-fold earth,
And of these there are six arch-demons, who
Soon formed a Council of Evil Beings:
The arch-demons Aka Manah, Indra,
Sauru, Zairitsha, Naonhaithya,
And Taurvi, the seventh being Aesthma
Or Ahriman, their Commander-in-Chief.
These demons gather at the door of Hell
In the mountain Aresura or in
The wild district of Mazandarin, south
Of the Caspian sea, and are drawn by
Impurity, and gather round a corpse.
Foremost is Aka Manah, evil mind,
And the Druj or Lie, the embodiment
Of the Evil Spirit Ahriman works,
Incarnation of that emanation.
And the Mesopotamians knew of

Mephistopheles, "he who does not love
Light" (Greek) or "destroyer-liar" (Hebrew).
Aesthma, the foul fiend of the wounding spear,
Is demon of wrath and fury; Azi
Dahaka, half-man, half-snake, wars against
Atar or Fire. The Greek evil demons,
Departed human spirits hostile to
The living who hovered in air and dwelt
Near Hades, the gods of the underworld,
Are winged Keres, who bring sorrow and
Mischief to men, blindness, madness, disease;
And daimons, intermediaries between
Gods and men, good ones who guard all men for
The gods and inspire them through oracles,
And spiteful, morally evil ones who
Lead men into unwholesome acts; harpies,
Winged wind-demons, women who snatch prey;
Gorgons who turn men to stone; sirens with
Fish-tails, mermaids who lure men with their songs;
Sphinxes, lion-women; and erinyes, dead
Outraged souls, ghosts crying out for vengeance.
The two hundred Angels who descended
On Mount Hermon, Senjaza, Azazel,
The unclean bird, the twelve-winged dragon,
And the rest, married the daughters of men
From lust, and fell and were bound by Michael
And Raphael; their children were giants who
Gave birth to a brood of evil spirits,
The Naphidim who seduced Noah's sons,
And Mastema's band of demons tempted
Abraham, the five Satans and their prince
Satanail, who was thrown down from the height
Of Heaven with his angels to fly above
The bottomless, also known as Satan,
Leader of Mastema, prince of evil
Spirits, and Beliar, prince of deceit
Who captured men through fornication and
Was with Sammael, dwelt in Manasseh's heart
Whose wantonness and worship of Satan
Drove Isaiah from Jerusalem. And
The New Testament evil or unclean
Spirits, demons and devils dwelt among
Wild beasts in waterless wildernesses,
And made men deaf, dumb, blind, epileptic
Or curved in spine, till Jesus rebuked them,

Exorcising them in profound belief
That Satan was the personal head of
The Kingdom of Evil opposed to God's
Reign in the trusting lives of pious men.

Above them all stood the Arch-Satan, the
Dark superhuman "adversary" who
Was an Angel of God, subordinate,
Unlike the independent Ahriman
Whom he claimed was a manifestation
(Deceitful as ever in his claimed powers),
Who opposed Ahura Mazda, the Light
While sharing in the work of creation,
For good Ahura Mazda had not caused
The cleavage between good and evil, which
Had arisen out of the universe.
Like the tempter of the Buddha, Mara,
Another of his manifestations,
Satan roamed through the earth on God's behalf
Like a Persian official the king sent,
And sought out acts or names he should report.
Satan first accused men before God and
Urged God to test men; thus he accused Job
Of selfish and insincere piety
And helped God prove that Job's piety was
Superficial, and, with God's permission,
Brought evils on Job to cause his downfall.
An Angel-minister of Yahweh, he
Appeared in Yahweh's presence, with the sons
Of Elohim, to report on his deeds
And to receive new divine commissions
Which were manifestations of God's will,
For Satan could not injure man unless
God allowed him to do so. But Satan
Also acted contrary to God's will
Which delighted in pious, perfect Job,
And tried to prove God's confidence in Job
Was misplaced; acting with God's permission,
He found joy in his anti-human work
And grew malignant and malevolent.
And, having vented his ill-will as Baal,
To oppose God's work by manifesting
As an idol who was loathsome to God,
Now he became a tempter with ill-will
And tempted David to number Israel's

Children and be punished by God, who may
Have commissioned Satan's dark spiteful test.
In Rabbinic texts Satan was Sammael,
The highest Throne-Angel, who had twelve wings,
Double the number of the Seraphim,
Who fell due to the Angels' jealousy.
Sammael, the first of the Angel princes,
Came down to earth and tempted restless Eve
To gain supremacy over mankind,
Revolted from the rule of God and led
A band of Angels into rebellion,
And then became accuser, seducer
And destroyer of Abraham, Isaac
And Sarah, and as Angel of Death caused
The death of Moses. Arch-Satan, chief of
Subordinate Satans, under God as
Angra Mainyu was under Ahura,
Then, tempted man as Angra tempted good
Zoroaster from his god Ahura;
Head of the kingdom of evil powers,
Of a host of evil spirits, Angels
Or demons hostile to both God and man,
Daevas. The Arch-Satan was created
By God, Jehovah, and had held his place
In the universe by God's permission
Whereas the Iranian Dark Spirit,
Self-originated Ahriman, claimed
To have an independent origin
Outside Ahura Mazda, though in fact
Non-Being emerged from the first Fire and
Cannot be said to be dualistic.
Good came from God through the Light of Being,
And evil came from Non-Being's Darkness
Which emerged from whole God to bring to birth
Being, its child from its Great Womb, its Void.
The Hebrew Satan became Greek Devil,
Another manifestation, deceit,
Diabolos, and evil spirits were
Daimons, departed human spirits who
Were hostile to the living. Five Satans
Who accused men in Heaven, and their prince
Satanail, instigated the revolt
Of the Angels and were thrown down from height
For refusing to worship the new man,
Adam, with Asmodeus, evil demon

Who slew Sarah's seven husbands. Of all,
The chief Satan, the Antichrist, the prince
Of Dan, God's enemy and man's, was worst.
He rampaged with the barbarians and
Sacked Rome to suffocate the Church. Michael
Fought back, and in the battle Satan was
Bound in a great chain for a thousand years
That he should deceive the nations no more
While Christ returned from Heaven and reigned on earth
For a millennium with his martyrs.
"As above, so below," Hermes' *Emerald*
Tablet declares. Now Christ's rule shone in the
Holy Roman Empire from Charlemagne
To Napoleon. Then Adam Weishaupt's
Illuminati merged with masonry
And loosed Satan to deceive the nations
In two world wars and more minor ones, and
Through Communism; slew the old order
To be behind the Antichrist, the man
Of lawlessness who would manifest as
The mighty ruler at the end of time
Who, at the head of gigantic armies,
Would destroy three rulers in the style of
Antiochus the Fourth, Epiphanes,
Or Nero, persecutors of the Jews,
Who resembled Hitler. At the end of
Armageddon, conflict between nations,
At the end of time, it is prophesied
That Satan will be cast into a lake
Of fire and brimstone forever, and that
All armies besieging "Jerusalem"
Will be devoured by fire from heaven, and,
In dreadful nuclear war, deceit will end,
And that the final destruction of Arch-
Satan will reverse the Age and bring in
A World Government of the Cosmic Christ
Whose Second Coming ushers an era
Of universal love and peace and hope.

The Cosmic Satan sat in his dark caves,
The Arch-enemy of God and man, who
Led the evil forces in the cosmos,
Master of all who are attached to sense,
On a ledge above the bottomless pit,
Full of deceit and aliases: Sammael,

Satanail, Devil, Dragon, Antichrist,
Angra Mainyu, Beliar, Abaddon,
Azazel, Serpent, Evil Mara, Beast,
Manichaean Prince of Darkness, Ruler
Of a Dark Kingdom he believed to be
Co-eval with the Light, whereas in fact
The latent Fire of Nothingness had borne
The first spiral of Darkness, Non-Being;
Mastema, Baal, Beelzebub, "lord of
The flies" and plagues, Baal-zebub god of
Ekron (to whom King Azakiah sent
To ask if he would survive his sickness),
Who could, like a chameleon, transform
Himself into an Angel of Light, grim
Disguise as Lucifer who he had been,
And hang upon the walls of Paradise,
Shine out and sing with the angelic hosts;
Cosmokrator, self-styled world-ruler, who
Believed he, not the Light, ruled all matter,
By wiles and snares seduced men to ruin
From loyalty to God, prince of the power
Of air, god of this Age with power of death,
Angel of Death, the evil one who could
Launch two hundred million demons at men
Who were alienated by their desires
From blissful union with the divine
And endured torments of meaninglessness,
And promote widespread disbelief in God;
Demons led by Abaddon, Apollyon,
Angel of the Abyss or lake of fire,
Final place of punishment for fallen
Angels, demons, and thousand-year prison
For Satan himself, which he dreamt he would
Reverse through a Reich that he mirrored in
Hitler's dream of a thousand-year Third Reich
On earth, and a thousand-year rule in Heaven.
Satan changed form to suit each occasion.
Now he was a dark shadow of black power,
Himself, a God-created force which drew
The dark demons like a magnet to him.
Sometimes they saw him in his most feared guise:
Instead of a bird of prey's great hooked bill
His long, horned, goat-like head like a vulture's
Sat between huge bat-like dragonish wings
Above Pan's cloven hoofs where claws were once,

Hybrid, mongrel, loathsome and repellent,
Hideous cross between a bird and beast,
More like a pterodactyl than a bat,
More like a vampire bat than a vulture,
More Pluto than Pan in his netherworld.
He was often a great red dragon with
Seven heads and ten horns, but most appeared
As an Angel of brilliant light, the bright
Lucifer, form acceptable to men.
Yet he could assume any form he chose,
And could impersonate any human,
Especially a nubile, curved woman.
But most often he took the form of man,
Of an international diplomat
In a suit, with glasses and receding
Hair, who might be seen at League of Nations
Or CFR conferences, or now
At UN, NATO, EU, Bilderberg,
CFR, Club of Rome, RIIA
Or Trilateral meetings; a highly
Paid functionary of the coming World
Government, Lord of the World in waiting,
Who seems a timeless mixture of Henry
Kissinger, Boutros Ghali, Jacques Delors
And Lord Carrington, all rational men
Who shaped our world with policies that failed,
Whose failures have torn Bosnia apart
And created a world that Satan wants,
Whose failures were in his terms successes,
Whose "failures" have put Hell in charge of us.
At that time Satan resembled several
Men who spoke for newsreels – Roosevelt, Truman,
Lord Halifax, Bevin, whoever spoke
For a UN (Rockefeller, Rothschild) –
So he could twist and pervert global work
Done by good, decent, well-intentioned men,
For, despite Satan's attempts to taint it,
World Government remains the best ideal.
When, Protean, he took a Dragon's shape
His physiognomy told the future
As he, deceitful, believed it would be:
Red for the Communist Red Flag, ten horns
For the regions of *his* World Government,
Seven heads for *his* Powers in the nations,
A Beast of a new order with shining

Luciferian masonic temples,
Dedicated to darkness, dressed in light;
But now a black shadow of towering height,
And before him like a swarm of locusts
Or like a seething sea of loathsome bats,
A black cloud of a billion Hellish things.

To this great bat-like throng in his caverns,
Informed by spies of the exclusion zone
Between the assembly point and Normandy,
Satan spoke: "Demons, hosts, powers of darkness,
Fallen Angels whose rightful place is Heaven,
We have long dreamt of reclaiming our land,
Of invading the Archangels' fortress
And overthrowing Michael and all those
Angels who chained us for a thousand years
Until our Illuminati agents
Freed us. Know that at last we now feel strong
Enough to attempt this revolution,
To challenge the leadership of Heaven,
To re-enter those gates we used to know
And capture the Angels and consign them
Here to this dark cavernous dungeon, and
Rule in triumph for ever, the bright earth
Ours. Our two allies Hitler and Stalin
Will together give us the world, for when
After this Armageddon, this great war,
This supreme conflict between the nations,
Hitler is the victor, he will possess
America, the British Empire, all
Soviet lands Stalin has united,
And we are strong in all three territories.
But foremost is the Master of the World,
The new world Messiah, the Antichrist,
Hitler, who derives energy from our
Great power. The three treacherous Allies have
At last invaded France, not where we thought,
Around Calais; the army near Dover
Was a sham one of cardboard and rubber,
To deceive the Nazis, and ourselves too.
So perfidious is Albion, so
Underhand and duplicitous. God and
His Archangels have once again stooped and
Compromised their dubious integrity
With a mean trick. They are in Normandy,

And have taken Hitler by surprise. Hosts,
Powers, *Angels*, we must now throw our support
On Hitler's side round Caen and rout the tanks
Of the Allies, throw them back to the sea.
This is the climax of Armageddon.
The treacherous Christ will be helping them,
And while his forces are engaged in France
We will seize our opportunity and
Have a lightning putsch on Heaven and take
Its citadels, force the transcendent God
To accept our immanent rule over
Both Heaven and earth, plan Hitler's victory,
And then, our fortunes changed, we can reflect
That this long exile in this loathsome place
Will have served its purpose and our brave cause,
To demonise mankind and to restore
Lucifer as the shining King of Heaven,
Take vengeance for this humiliation.
Buzz if you approve this brilliant idea."
And when he finished a loud buzzing rose
As if a billion flies, large bluebottles,
And half a billion wasps on a window
Fanned their transparent wings in unison,
And their approval was like a "Sieg heil"
In Nuremberg, or applause in Red Square,
For Satan's rule was a dictatorship,
The model for Hitler's and Stalin's rule,
And his decision, deceitful decree,
Announced in speech, could not be voted on.

Unaware of war between Heaven and Hell
But preoccupied with his own conflict
And dereliction of duty that had
Found him absent from his post at H-Hour,
Rommel arrived at La Roche Guyon at
Nine-thirty; Speidel saluted. He heard
Of the immense armada from the sea,
How 21st Panzers had lost thirteen
Tanks near Hermanville, that the Orne bridges
Had fallen to airborne assault, and that
The enemy were six miles inland for
A stretch of ten miles, shallow beachheads past
The Atlantic Wall, which in Normandy was
Only one fifth built. His underwater
Obstacles had hardly delayed the craft,

And though some were holed by mines and steel, and
Strongpoints had pinned many invaders down,
France had been successfully invaded,
The enemy had not been defeated
On the beaches, as was his strategy.
Rommel sat at his desk and pondered that
This was a diversion, the main attack
Would come in the Pas de Calais.
The larger the diversion was, the more
Credible. But even if the main thrust
Was still to come, Germany was now faced
With a land war on two fronts, east and west,
And this augured disaster in the field.

At the Berghof, alone on D-Day night,
Like a shaman Hitler withdrew to hear
Prophesying voices in mountain quiet,
Within his head, that altered consciousness
By ritual magic, and to pour their power
Into the doubting stagnant German soul
From whose well, in turn, he drew energy
Along with what he received from Satan,
Antichrist who possessed him like a slave
So he was a puppet to Satan's whim,
A sleepwalker, a medium possessed,
A hypnotised man in a trance, dreaming
Voices that babbled increase in the war.
Hitler held the spear of Longinus, which
Was brought to him from Nuremberg Castle.
Made by Phineas, the Old Testament
Prophet, to symbolise the magic powers
In the Jewish blood, it had been raised by
Joshua when the walls of Jericho
Crumbled before a shout; it had been hurled
By Saul at David. Herod Antipas
Held it while he ordered the massacre
Of the innocent babes of Judaea
To kill the Christ child who would be "King of
The Jews". Caiaphas and Annas ordered
The mutilation of Christ's body to
Show he was not the Messiah, and sent
The Temple Guard, whose Captain held the spear
As Herod's son's authority to act.
Gaius Cassius Longinus held the sponge
Dipped in vinegar on the spear for Christ

To drink, and when Christ died he was repelled
By the Guard's cruel smashing of the skulls
Of the two thieves, Gestas and Dismas, and
Out of compassion for Christ's dead body,
Being partly Teutonic, he charged his
Horse at Christ's cross and thrust his spear between
The fourth and fifth ribs on his right side to
Prove he was dead; and as blood and water
Flowed, his failing sight was restored, and he
Witnessed the blood of the New Covenant
Which streamed to the earth, containing spirit
That incarnated as the cosmic Christ,
The spirit-essence in the Holy Blood.
At once Longinus became a Christian.
The spear which pierced the side of Christ and which
Bore witness to the crucifixion was
The greatest treasure in Christendom, and
The legend grew that whoever owned it
Held the destiny of the world, for good
Or evil; its claimant could choose to serve
Opposing spirits, one good, one evil.
Constantine the Great felt he was guided
By Providence as he held the spear at
The battle of Milvian Bridge, near Rome.
Theodosius tamed the Goths with it.
Alaric claimed it after he sacked Rome.
Aetius, last of the Romans, and the great
Visigoth Theodoric held it when
They turned back Attila the Hun at Troyes.
Justinian raised it when he ordered
The closure of the schools of Athens, which
Reopened as Ficino's Platonic
Academy in Medici Florence.
Charles Martel, who reunited the Franks,
Drove the Saracens from Poitiers with it.
Charlemagne attributed forty-seven
Victories to its powers, and founded his
Dynasty on it, and kept it in reach.
Forty-five Emperors held it for a
Thousand years. Heinrich the Fowler founded
The Saxon dynasty with it, his son
Otto the Great knelt before the Pope to
Be touched by it and be Holy Roman
Emperor. Frederick the Second took
It on crusades, Francis of Assisi

Once carried it. The Teutonic Knights were
Founded with it. The Hohenstauffens held
It, including Barbarossa, and then
The Habsburgs. Napoleon asked for it
At Austerlitz. It was in Vienna
In the Habsburgs' Hofburg Treasury that
Hitler first saw it, aged fifteen. Four years
Later he saw his future before it
And longed one day to possess it so he
Might dominate the world. Through Eckart, he
Had opened his centres to Lucifer,
And his halting speech would suddenly be
Taken over by a magical flow
Of words as he channelled demonic power
And was possessed by superhuman force
From the Antichrist, hatred of the Jews
That made him excited, left him worn out.
He knew Nietzsche's *Genealogy of*
Morals, which "proved" Christian good is evil
And Christian evil good; and *Antichrist*,
Which challenged the Christians; and Schopenhauer's
The World as Will and Idea, which held that
Conceptual thought could not attain to truth,
That only the experience of willpower
Approached reality. He had read of
The Superman, and man's overcoming;
How God is dead and all is will to Power.
He knew Wagner, whose *Parsival* shows that
In the hands of Parsival, the Grail Knight,
The spear symbolises the blood of Christ,
But in the grasp of Klingsor in the south
It was a phallic wand with black magic
Powers. Two forces flow round the earth, and are
Drawn to the spear, and its owner opens
To one of them, aware the spear bridges
The world of sense and the world of spirit.
Hitler opened to the spear's dark force; and,
Guided, "moving like a sleep-walker where
Providence dictated", he groped towards
Personal power, tyranny, world conquest.
In place of the Christian view that it showed
Christ overcoming Satan-Ahriman,
Hitler saw the spear as a symbol of
The battle between Light and Dark above
And between good and evil here below,

In which Dark pierced the side of Light and won.
Twenty-five years later Hitler owned it,
And lodged it at Nuremberg so it could
Spread evil into the Nazi movement.
In the Berghof he felt the black metal
That had been covered with the blood of Christ,
Invoked the talisman by his willpower,
Appealed to Satan through his magic art
To send a current of hostility
At Eisenhower, the Supreme Commander
Of Allied troops, his main adversary,
And vowed he would repel Montgomery
And the "evil" forces of Christendom
Which he would strike with a thrust of his spear.
In his hand he held a rod, he thought, that
Directed Satan's lightning at his foes.

Tired and depressed after the tension and
Then his elation at the beach landings,
Eisenhower sat in his trailer, hidden,
Like an owl watching from a hollow tree,
In woods, and smoked, waiting for new reports
From the front, and each time the telephone
Rang he grabbed it. In turns he smiled or frowned,
Smiled when he heard that Bayeux was falling,
Frowned when he learned that Caen was resisting.
Kay rang the mess, and sandwiches were brought
For supper; she boiled water for coffee
On a small spirit stove. They stayed quite late,
Waiting for one more report to come through,
Until, tired and listless, they went to bed.
Then Eisenhower lay and in his mind flew
Over the hedgerows of Normandy and
Saw soldiers lying in foxholes they'd dug
Or covered with an eiderdown of leaves,
Sleeping like slithering things close to the earth.
He felt their cold, their damp, knew their quiet fear.

Next dawn the Luftwaffe bombed the beaches,
And there were a few counter-attacks by
The Germans. The troops had slept little as
The wounded had to be carried to ships,
The dead buried, obstacles cleared from sand.
Patrols went out into the dark. On board

HMS Faulknor, Montgomery told
Bradley all beaches must link up, all men
Must keep moving forward. Eisenhower
Left Portsmouth and conferred on *Apollo*
With his commanders, and looked from the deck
As the minelayer hugged the Normandy
Coastline. Cautious Montgomery spoke: "Ike,
The immediate tactical plan has
Been altered on the whole US Army
Front, as the American problem on
Omaha beach makes it vital Utah
And Omaha troops link up." Eisenhower,
Sitting on the deck of the great ship, said,
"All right, I will signal the Combined Chiefs
Of Staff in Washington that after that
Adjustment, the original conceptions
Will be pursued." And he added, "Monty,
I am concerned Caen has not been captured."
Cautious Montgomery said, "It is clear
That the enemy intend to hold it
Strongly and drive into my eastern flank.
Dempsey will have to envelop Caen, not
Take it by a frontal attack, and then
Pivot on Caen and swing his right flank as
The plan provides. I am well satisfied
With today's fighting." Butcher glowered, for he
Resented the Commander-in-Chief's smug
Self-satisfaction. When Montgomery
Had gone he said, "He made out that his plan
Was messed up by Americans, and seemed
To derive secret satisfaction from
Rearranging the American front."
Eisenhower shrugged.
Rommel sent German tanks
To drive between forces coming ashore
Off the beaches, and stormed Ste Mère-Eglise,
Where they were repelled. British troops entered
Bayeux, Germans took Merville battery
And shelled Sword beach. Sword and Juno linked up,
But 21st and 12th Panzers again
Halted the British before Caen, to their
Relief, a smoking wall that rolled slowly
Like volcano lava and pressed them back
Towards the sea. They fought between two floods,
The Dives on the east, and west, the Douve

With green and open water-meadows, swamps.
Inland, cow pastures and orchards, earthbanks
Topped with hedgerows, and sunken lanes with banks
Or stone walls, and farmhouses: the bocage
From Cotentin to Falaise, hedgerows, hills,
Streams and villages, Norman-towered churches.
Overlooked, the Americans fought in
The hedgerows, knowing the Overlord plan
Had Caen falling on D-Day, to the west
A low hill, to the east a sloping plain,
An open place of death with no cover.

Montgomery landed, his TAC HQ,
Three caravans, stopped near Ste Croix-sur-Mer
At a crossroads, then drove to a château
At Creullet, which Warren, his Canadian
Assistant had found occupied by some
Fifteen Germans, whom he took prisoner.
He asked Mme de Druval, gesturing,
For a chamber-pot. She brought vases, then
A magnificent pot whose large crest said
"Montgomery". Sitting in a soft chair
By his caravans, Montgomery told
A BBC newsman: "My ancestors
Came from Ste Foy de Montgomery, near
Falaise. Sir Roger de Montgomery,
My forebear, was William the Conqueror's
Second-in-Command when the Norman ships
Invaded Britain, and he left Falaise
Near where Duke Robert saw Arlette washing
Clothes in a stream and fathered the bastard
William, to whom Edward promised England –
Till perjurer Harold usurped his crown,
And so he sailed from Dives with his fleet
As told in the Bayeux Tapestry. My
Family invaded Britain, and now
Are liberating the Conqueror's land
From the Saxon yoke. I have presided
Over a British conquest of the land
Of the Normans, a reverse take-over."

Eisenhower, back in his trailer, waited
For reports with Kay. He held press briefings,
Answered cables of congratulation,
Saw de Gaulle and Churchill, studied reports,

Urged commanders to double their efforts.
Each other day Kay drove him to London,
And Bushey Park and Telegraph Cottage,
Each night she drove him back to Portsmouth so
He could see the latest message. Cautious
Montgomery signalled that Dempsey would
Strike south of Caen at Villers-Bocage while
The Americans linked their two beachheads.
The next night he received no signal from
Montgomery, and next morning left his
HQ in a rage, complaining "Monty
Promised to cable every night." He wished
To be field commander, run 21st
Army Group, know the latest from the front.
Moody, he would become depressed, and then
Turn optimistic, seize on the hopeful,
Impatient for news from the battlefield.
The signal was found in Most Secret code,
It explained how Montgomery planned to
Surround Rommel's entire force of Panzers
In a pincer movement, with paratroops,
South of Caen. Now Eisenhower's quick mind
Anticipated success, buoyed him up,
And the German counter-attacks were good
As they assembled tanks in Monty's trap.
He learned that Bradley had at last now linked
The Utah and Omaha beachheads, and
That Collins was racing for Cherbourg, that
Without American help, the British
Desert Rats were advancing near Tilly
To seize Villers-Bocage, the same troops who
Fought with Montgomery at Alamein
And defeated Rommel. In hopeful mood,
Buoyed up and confident, he understood
That Montgomery's strategy, outlined
In May, was to pull the Germans onto
The British left, which would stop them at Caen,
So the American right could break out
From Cherbourg and surround them from the rear,
As a boxer blocks his opponent's punch
With his left glove, then swings a right hook to
His jaw, which knocks him out. But when depressed
He thought Montgomery had failed at Caen –
It was the main objective on D-Day –
And that he rationalised failure when he

Said he had never planned to capture Caen.

Four days after D-Day Hitler sat in
The Berghof with Göring and Dönitz, who
Told him, "The invasion has succeeded,
The Second Front has come." The Overlord
Of Europe stared accusingly till they
Looked down, uncomfortable. The chiefs of air
And sea blamed each other. Göring declared,
"The Navy assured us the enemy
Would not risk his best ships in a seaborne
Invasion." Dönitz replied, "There should be
More air strikes, against the enemy's ten
Thousand on invasion day, our Luftwaffe
Flew only three hundred." Hitler then spoke
And both were respectfully silent. "I
Have warned since March that the first invasion
Would come in Normandy, not near Calais.
No one listened to me." He gave orders
That 9th and 10th Panzers should now be sent
To the Normandy front. Burgdorf, his chief
Adjutant, spoke: "Rommel plans to divert
His counter-attack from the British force
Driving on Caen to the American
Advance on Cherbourg, then return to stop
Dempsey's advance towards Villers-Bocage."
Bormann, Hitler's cunning Chief of Party
Chancellery, like a devil at his ear,
Dropping his voice, confiding, said, "Rommel
Is letting the British advance on Caen."
Hitler frowned and spoke: "Caen's nearer Paris
Than Cherbourg. I veto Rommel's plan; send
Rommel an Enigma signal, Army
Group B will attack the British from Caen."
And all the Generals nodded their assent,
Aware that their positions required it.

The Utah and Omaha troops linked up
When Screaming Eagles attacked through hedgerows
Round Carentan, all night artillery,
Mortar and naval fire blasted the dark.
The Germans withdrew south, the paratroops
Took the town and secured their line. Next day
The Germans counter-attacked but could not
Break through, and one American force looked

Towards St. Lô and now exposed Cherbourg.

As he received Churchill, Smuts and Brooke at
His tactical HQ at Creullet, while
Bradley received General Marshall, the boss
Of Eisenhower, Montgomery knew from
Ultra intercepts that three more Panzer
Divisions were on their way to Caen, and
That the Desert Rats should beat them to Caen.
The VIPs lunched in his tent, three miles
From the German front line, and then they went
Into the Operations trailer for
A talk on strategy, and he described
The British left parry, US right hook,
And stressed, "The Allied aim is to defeat
The German Armies in the West, not to
Break out towards the Seine." Later he thanked
Brooke for supporting him in London with
Churchill and Tedder, and, alone, they talked
Of Eisenhower. Montgomery said, "His
Approach to war differs from my approach.
He is pulling against me all the time."
Brooke said, "His friendly exterior hides
A ruthless mind that balances national
Interests and leads by compromise. He is
Restless, he latches on to new ideas,
And integrates them in his military
Scheme. He is easy-going – that alarmed
Our Cabinet – and reads western novels,
But he is a great man, like Caesar or
William the Conqueror, who reminds me
Of a fox. After he was appointed –
He got the job because Roosevelt would not
Release General Marshall, his Chief of Staff –
He hoped Alexander would have your job,
But he is as easy-going as Ike,
And I, for one, voted for you. And then
You ripped to pieces the COSSAC plan he
Had approved. You must expect him to be
Difficult sometimes." The VIPs left,
And Montgomery heard Leigh-Mallory
Was not keen to drop paratroops near Caen
Lest Allied ships fired at his planes at night.

The Desert Rats entered Villers-Bocage

Between the Germans defending Caen and
The Germans facing the Americans.
The tanks drove through on the Caen road, the first
Four stopped to wait for the rest to catch up,
The crews got out. Five Tiger tanks, Panzers,
Lay in wait, under Michael Wittmann of
The Waffen-SS, the ace who destroyed
A hundred and thirty-eight Russian tanks
And held the record for the most tanks put
Out of action on either side. Alone,
He set off across the fields and destroyed
Four Cromwells in the village further back,
Blocking the road and retreat. He returned
To the Tigers, and they went down the line
Just as a shooting party encounter
A colony of pheasant on the ground
And shoot and bag the lot with scornful stealth,
And soon destroyed twenty-seven tanks and
Twenty-eight armoured vehicles. Later that
Day his tank returned, but was disabled –
It lost a track to an anti-tank gun –
And he withdrew. The British then pulled back
From Villers-Bocage, and the drive on Caen
Was stopped. Rommel, defying Hitler, pushed
Westwards, and took Carentan. Archangel
Michael saw, and was concerned that Rommel
Had given Montgomery's Desert Rats
A bloody nose and pushed them back from Caen.
Out of the sky came the first of Hitler's
Reprisal weapons, V-1s or buzz-bombs,
Droning in the sky like a wasp and then
Silent as its engine cut out and fell.
A loud crash, a crater in Bethnal Green,
And fear as all looked at the skies and cowered
And listened for the drone and then silence.
Eisenhower had feared that the buzz-bombs
Would have atomic warheads. He had been
Warned by Alsos – Bush, Goudsmit and Groves – and
When the first V-1 fell, Goudsmit measured
The crater for radioactivity
With a Geiger counter and found no trace.
Eisenhower was relieved and told Stimson.

As Eisenhower sat in the SHAEF office
At 20 Grosvenor Square in London

On the day of the first buzz-bomb and stared,
His newly graduated son, sent by
Marshall, John, a tall second lieutenant,
Walked in, threw his arms round him and kissed him
On his cheek. Eisenhower grinned and proudly
Showed him round headquarters, then Kay drove them
To Telegraph Cottage where they talked most
Of the night. (Kay left at midnight.) John was
Unassuming and correct, as charming
As his father, who could be critical,
As when John complained of a restless night
On the bare springs of a mattressless cot
Before his graduation, the night of
D-Day, and Eisenhower looked stern, then grim,
But said nothing, thinking of all the men
Sleeping in French foxholes or near beaches
Without the luxury of a mattress.
John soon liked Kay, and saw how popular
She was, and how relaxed his father was
With her. He wanted to see Normandy,
Where Montgomery was no nearer Caen.

At SHAEF HQ Eisenhower, impatient,
Complained to Bedell Smith, his Chief of Staff,
"What's the matter with Monty? Why won't he
Attack? The Germans should be off balance,
But he needs supplies, and does not make gains
And even retreats. He has not taken
The airfields south of Caen as he promised
Leigh-Mallory, and the air commanders
At this morning's meeting spoke of 'a state
Of crisis'. Even Tedder says that 'the
Present situation has the makings
Of a dangerous crisis'." He resolved
To see the battle zone himself with John
And Tedder. The next morning they flew in,
Escorted by thirteen well-armed fighters,
And drove to Bayeux, the home of William
The Conqueror, and thence out to Creullet
"To see if there really is a crisis".

The previous day, having received de Gaulle,
Who had landed at Courseulles as leader
Of the Free French and wanted to have charge
Of liberated land, and was told No,

Montgomery had seen Leigh-Mallory,
Who had visited Creullet and offered
A bombing raid along a front, behind
Which the army could advance. They agreed
The details should be worked out the next day
Between Leigh-Mallory's planning staff and
Dempsey's. Leigh-Mallory flew back and rang
Coningham, who phoned Tedder and complained.
When Eisenhower and Tedder reached Creullet
They were informed Montgomery had left
To tour the American sector with
Bradley, and would not be back until four.
Eisenhower blamed himself for short notice,
Tedder smarted at what he called a snub.
Together they went to Dempsey's HQ
And found the Army/Air conference that
Leigh-Mallory had promised, in session,
Discussing heavy bombing support for
Ground troops. Coningham happened to arrive
By chance, or so was said, and, egged on by
Tedder and Coningham, Eisenhower told
Dempsey that Leigh-Mallory had not told
SHAEF about Bomber Command's air support
With 8 US AF for infantry,
Which could not work; and sent the airmen home.

Montgomery returned to his Creullet
And found, sitting in his mess tent, his own
Supreme Commander and his Deputy,
Wise Eisenhower and treacherous Tedder.
He greeted Eisenhower's son, who then left
The tent, and Eisenhower said, "We arrived
This morning, as you should have known. Finding
You gone, we visited Dempsey's HQ
And found an Army/Air conference there."
Montgomery explained Leigh-Mallory's
Offer, but Tedder interrupted: "I
Was concerned as Spatz and Coningham were
Not represented. We are sure that air
Bombing cannot support ground attacks, so
We have sent the airmen home, the idea
Is dropped." Montgomery stared at Tedder.
He began to object, but, grasping that
The issue was not simply military,
He said, "Then the armies must fight Rommel

Without the support of heavy bombers,
Without *all* weapons in SHAEF's arsenal."
Inside his Operations caravan
He briefed them on his plan: "I must stress, Caen
Is the key to Cherbourg. Rommel must be
Made to believe, and Hitler too, that the
British are attempting to break out in
The east towards the Seine, so they dare not
Release the four Panzer divisions to
Block the American thrust to Cherbourg.
Villers-Bocage has helped them believe that.
It has not imperilled Bradley's drive, but
Is the key to its success." He spoke well,
With great clarity, while wise Eisenhower
Took notes on the supplies Montgomery
Required, ammunition and fresh fighting
Divisions. Clear Montgomery said, "My
Normandy strategy is succeeding."
Eisenhower said, "Monty, we are impressed,
There is no crisis." Now not arrogant
For once, Tedder said, "The military
Crisis was over-emphasised." They went,
But Eisenhower, impatient at the lack
Of gains, disappointed and restless, turned
His attention to Anvil, the invasion
Around Bordeaux, not challenging Tedder's
Opposition to bomber help with air
Commanders, concerned to keep consensus.

Hitler and his staff flew to Metz in four
Focke-Wulf Condor aircraft. All Luftwaffe
Fighter units were grounded, and anti-
Aircraft batteries were shut down. Next day
Hitler drove to Margival, near Soissons;
The Luftwaffe gave air cover above
The highway and an unseen escort flew
Behind his car, of Satan's emissaries.
Wolfschlucht 2 was built as Hitler's command
Post for his planned invasion of England.
This was his first visit to it. Still tired,
He crouched on his stool, in a bad mood as
The Allies were advancing through North France,
And fumbled with his glasses and pencils
Near Jodl, Schmundt, Buhle and stenographers.
Rommel and Rundstedt sat with Chiefs of Staff

And Hitler spoke robustly: "You allowed
The enemy invasion to succeed.
You are incompetent." Rommel explained
The enemy and German positions
On a map, and said, "Our troops are fighting
To the last breath, but lack air cover and
Are in a one-sided struggle that is
Hopeless. As in Africa, the Allies
Have material superiority."
Rundstedt said, "I have asked permission to
Withdraw troops from the northern Cotentin
Peninsula towards Cherbourg fortress."
Hitler spoke: "The Cotentin will be cut
In two. Cherbourg must hold out until mid-
July, to hinder the enemy's new
Supplies through the port there, which are crucial.
We will mine the coast and stop sea-supply.
The enemy's most experienced troops
Are now in Normandy, this invasion
Is not a mere diversion, we must hold
Cherbourg." Rommel said: "It is senseless to
Hold fortresses to the last man. We need
Troops, tanks, air cover and naval support,
And our Panzers must be kept away from
Naval gunfire." Hitler spoke of his new
Secret weapons, flying bombs, jet fighters.
Two hundred and forty-four V-1s were
Being fired at London that day. Rommel
And Rundstedt asked for flying bombs to be
Sent against the Allied beachheads. Hitler
Refused, as their inaccuracy might
Endanger German troops. He said, "But soon,
Soon I will have an atomic bomb that
Will pulverise the Allied armies and
Reduce London to rubble with one blast
And win the war for us." Air-raid sirens
Wailed the approach of enemy aircraft.
All went to the air-raid shelter, Hitler
And Rommel stood together, and Rommel
Said, "I predict the Wehrmacht will collapse
On all fronts and that Germany will be
Politically isolated. It
Is time to end the war." Hitler rebuked
Him: "That has nothing to do with you. Your
Business is to resist the invasion.

It is not time for a political
Decision, for one sues for peace from strength.
To sue now would be to admit defeat.
My V-1s will make Britain sue for peace.
Concern yourself with military matters,
Not political considerations."
And Rommel left, buoyed up by Hitler's power,
The sheer magnetism of his great will,
But also feeling as if a chasm
Had widened in his trust of the Führer,
Who, planning to drive to La Roche Guyon,
Was badly shaken when a flying bomb
With apparently defective steering,
But in fact guided by the Christ's Angels,
Crashed above his bunker, with the result
That he drove straight home to Berchtesgaden.

Satan's forces raised a great wind, seeking
To disrupt the Allies' supplies, and soon
A ferocious storm lashed the heaving sea,
The worst storm in living memory, which
Sank or damaged more ships than the Germans
Did in the entire North West Europe campaign.
The Mulberry harbours, towed into place in
Sections that were bolted together, rose
And fell. The British harbour held fast, but
The American harbour smashed, sunken
Transport ships acted as breakwaters, and
Convoys were driven home, small craft were lost,
Eight hundred craft beached for a month. The storm
Raged furiously, and the sea was so
Violent that few tanks or trucks were landed,
Only a third of unloadings took place.
A hurricane whipped up mountainous waves,
And as Hitler had promised, the Allies
Could not supply their armies from the sea.
Hitler said, "It's divine intervention."
He deceived himself by confusing the
Divine with the infernal, wanting to
Believe he was an agent for much good,
Believing that evil is a good power.
Montgomery, watching the lashing rain
From his caravan, ruefully announced,
"Normandy is known as 'le peau de chambre',
The chamber-pot, because it is a bowl

That collects so much rain when it is wet."
The Allies needed a port to unload
Their supplies and transport, and Collins cut
Off the Cotentin peninsula and
Attacked Cherbourg from the landward side with
Support from air and naval bombardments.
When they captured the port and von Schlieben
Surrendered, the Allies found it so well
Demolished it was useless for a month.
The only ports were still Mulberries and beaches.

Tell, Muse, how Hitler and Himmler took part
In Aryan Iranian fire rites
That drew on Satan's power and trampled Christ.
There are two forces that may seem the same,
That fill the "dualistic" universe:
The high soul-energy that comes from God,
The Light, the universal energy
That is known in gnosis and brings wisdom,
Guidance, healing and serene calm within;
And the low earth-energy from Satan
That can be used by the will for magic,
Can be harnessed, controlled by rituals.
Mystic power is higher than psychic force.
In woodland at Verden, Himmler decreed
That four thousand five hundred standing stones
Should commemorate where Charlemagne killed
As many Saxons. Avenues open
Into stone circles. Here in December
Nazis gathered for pagan ritual
At the winter solstice, under Himmler:
The birth of the sun child from the ashes
Of Jesus Christ, an anti-Christian feast
Poached from the Order of the Golden Dawn
To which Beast Crowley, 666, belonged,
From which Hitler took the raised arm salute.
Now this dark summer solstice before dawn
Ten thousand uniformed cult-Nazis burned,
By torchlight, an effigy of Jesus
As symbol of the Allies and the Christ,
And watched the sun rise over the menhirs
(Fake prehistory built at Himmler's command)
As at Stonehenge. Here the Cross of Christ was
The symbol of the sun-god: vertical
Between summer and winter solstices,

Horizontal between the vernal and
Autumnal equinox – the sun's farthest
And nearest points to the equator, caught
In the rotation of the swastika.
Here the Order of new Templars, structured
Just like the Society of Jesus
(Himmler himself being called "Loyola"),
The SS, worshipped, through the sun and fire,
The force that fills the universe with power,
Which can be controlled by the personal will
In rituals which produce a force and give
A magical effect, psychic white light,
A field of energy that can be tapped
By the lower will, which follows ley-lines
And can be manipulated for ill
By those who follow Darkness and oppose
The true mystic Light of both God and Christ
To which we subordinate our desires.
The Devil's way is through the human will
While God's way involves its subjugation.
Here was to be born a new world order
That would vanquish the old order we know,
The Christian-humanistic tradition.
Here occult invocation, ritual chants
By thousands of torch-holding uniformed
Men raised all-pervading earth-energy
Whose mastery gives unlimited power;
The universal force called Vril which spread
Its energy-system across Europe
And could be known in mountain top rituals,
On holy mountains like the Eagle's Nest.
After the First World War Hitler became
A police agent in Munich, where he
Spied on secret societies and soon
Infiltrated occult-political
Groups thought subversive, one of which was the
German Workers' Party, led by Dietrich
Eckart, racist magician and poet.
This group was mystical, and Hitler joined
On Reichswehr Intelligence's orders
And renamed it in a Hofbrauhaus speech
The National Socialist German Workers'
Party, Nazi for short. Eckart led the
Thule Society, which sought the Nordic
Home, Thule. He prayed to a black stone and, like

Theosophists, "Powers" in Tibet. Through him
And others Hitler contacted a power
Linked with Landulf the Second's Satanic
Practices at Caltabellotta (called
Kalot Enbolot by Eschenbach) where,
In an Arab-occupied Sicily,
The ninth century Landulf invoked spirits
Of darkness through torture and sacrifice.
Eckart had found the castle, where Crowley
Invoked the Beast, the Apocalyptic
Spirit, the Antichrist, which appeared to
Pretzsche and List, Eckart and Rosenberg,
The Luciferic Leviathan which
Possessed the body and soul of Hitler.
Eckart seems to have tried such Satanic
Vile practices on Jews and Communists.
He had initiated Hitler, who
Thought he was once Landulf of Capua,
And was a Satanist in Sicily,
That he reincarnated as Wagner's
Bishop Klingsor, the Count of Acerra,
Duke of Terra di Labur or Capri
(Where Hitler tried to buy Tiberius'
Temple to retire to in his old age),
An adept of magic and the black arts
Who died in eleven ninety-seven.
Hitler now opened to Satanic power,
A dark earth-energy, a chthonic force,
The Vril known to the Vril Society
Or sect, whose symbol was the swastika,
Which through Jacolliot's universal
Vril, synthesised Swedenborg, Boehme and
The Bavarian Illuminati,
Who reappeared in eighteen eighty through
Leopold Engel, founder of the British
Hermetic Order of the Golden Dawn.
This Vril was known to several occult sects:
The Theosophical Society
Of Blavatsky, an initiate in
Mazzini's Carbonari, and therefore
The Illuminati who ran them both;
Von List's magical order Armanen;
Stauff's breakaway Germanen Order, and
Von Sebbottendorf's inner movement in
It, the Premier Antisemitic Lodge;

The Thule Society whose sword, oak leaves
And curved swastika became Nazi lore
And which was the "Black Order" ("Schwarze Orden");
Lanz von Liebenfels's New Templars, whose
Banner was a swastika and who met
Hitler in nineteen nine, who wrote twenty-
Three years later, "Hitler is one of our
Pupils" and "he, and through him, we will one
Day... develop a movement that will make
The world tremble"; also the Order of
Eastern Templars of Reuss, who met Crowley
Before the Great War, which practised the arts
Of the magical Illuminati
And accepted Crowley's prose-poem, *The
Book of the Law* and the religion of
Crowley's Abbey of Thelema in which
Daemonic forces would smash rational power,
And which split into factions, one of which
Followed Crowley, led by Marthe Kuntzel
Who sent Hitler *The Book of the Law* and
Made him her pupil and "magical child",
Crowley swore, so Hitler's ideas were shaped
From nineteen twenty-five by Crowley's *Book*
And the earthbound spirits of Black Magic;
And Keyserling's School of Wisdom. Eckart,
Thulean and Nazi, as he died of drink
(Some said of drugs or a sexual disease)
Spoke thus: "Follow Hitler. He will dance but
It is I who have called the tune. I have
Initiated him in the Secret
Doctrine, opened his centres of vision
And given him the means to communicate
With the Powers. Do not mourn me, for I
Shall have influenced history more than
Any other German." Through the Thule came
Theosophy's awareness of Aryan
Purity in India and Iran:
Sanskrit swastika and Mazdaism,
Worship of Ahura Mazda, the god
Of Light, whose eye is the sun, who later
Combined with Spenta Mainyu as Ohramazd.
Through the Thule came Hitler's dualism,
His Gnostic belief in the dark and light,
His Manichaeism and his Cathar

Belief the Devil created the world,
Dark Ahriman, Rex Mundi, equal in
Power and status to God, who was above
The world; and that demiurge Jehovah
Is this Ahriman, and must be opposed
By the god Mazda with his eagle wings,
Who visited the high up Eagle's Nest.
In nineteen forty-two, Hitler had made
(So he professed, Mazda was but a mask)
A Faust-like pact with the Wise Lord, Mazda:
Blood sacrifice to trap the Vril that would
Make him Lord of the World. And at Verden,
A magician who worked its energy,
Having reversed the Aryan swastika –
From Krohn's right-handed to left-handed form,
From good fortune and triumph of spirit
To bad luck and triumph of dark power like
Black Mass reversal of a crucifix –
So his Nazi symbol stood for evil,
He invoked the help of the Aryan god,
To whom the Nazis sacrificed with fire –
The torches of Nuremberg rallies and
The smoking furnaces of Auschwitz –
And in return received, he now believed
(Or so he claimed to those who questioned him),
Ahura Mazda's inspired truth and light,
But in fact received Ahriman's dark power
As Landulf, Eckart, Crowley would have known.
So Satan deceived him into thinking
That his occult energy was divine,
It might be charitably said – or so
He knowingly used Mazda as a mask
And hid Satan's power, calling it "divine",
When he opposed Jehovah for Satan.
Though his Nazi Order opposed masons
As well as Christians and purged all secret
Societies except the SS Knights
Of the Round Table at Schloss Wewelsburg,
Hitler was a secret follower of
The Bavarian Illuminati –
Who opposed Christianity but based
Their organisation on Jesuits,
On structured progress from novice to priest,
As did the SS Black Order – and he

Concealed their Satanist beliefs as did
Satan himself, who called demons "Angels".

Eisenhower, wanting constant attack at
Each point along the line, like General Grant
In the Virginia Wilderness in
The American Civil War, saw Caen
Hold out in German hands and heard the news
Of the great storm by phone at Telegraph
Cottage. "I need a drink," he said, "more Scotch.
Kay, if we had postponed D-Day, today
Was the next possible date. We have been
Saved from a disaster." The flying bombs
Disturbed his nights; now he slept in the mound
In the garden, the shelter Churchill built,
With John and Kay and four staff cramped in close.
SHAEF HQ in London was abandoned
When a roof was blown from a corridor.
Eisenhower set up an Advance Command
Post in Portsmouth, and impotently watched
Montgomery's slow progress around Caen,
Which could not be destroyed in a frontal
Attack as there were French inhabitants;
The obstacle which pinned the British near
Their beaches, and blocked any move inland.
After two diversionary assaults
Dempsey attacked from the west, bagpipers
Playing; in mist and frowning clouds sixty
Thousand troops with tanks and flame-throwers fought
Across cornfields, where steel helmets rested
On rifles stuck, bayonet down, in the earth,
And in pouring rain across the Odon.
The British held the northern hill, the south
Slopes were in German hands, in torrential
Rain they fired mortars and artillery
At each other for two days. Then arrived
Two SS Panzer divisions from the
Eastern front. Ultra warned the Allies, and
Heavy bombers bombed Villers-Bocage, while
Artillery, air power, infantry and
Tanks stopped the Waffen-SS. Dempsey pulled
Back from Hill 112, his drive halted.
Eisenhower fumed: there was no way to Caen
From the west. All along his plan had been
To land enough troops and thrust far enough

Inland by the end of June so that Twelfth
Army Group could be formed under Bradley
And he could take command of the battle.
Montgomery's lack of progress delayed
The forming of Bradley's Group and therefore
Eisenhower's command, and it seemed at SHAEF
That a British General was losing a
Battle fought with American lives and
Equipment, while being arrogant to
His subordinates and ignoring his
Superiors. Montgomery, unlike
Haig in the First World War, tried not to risk
His troops' lives and proceeded with caution.

Worried by the surrender of Cherbourg,
Rommel asked Rundstedt if he could talk with
Hitler, Arch-Satan's ally, Overlord.
Rommel spoke to von Rundstedt near Paris:
"I agree, the war must be ended now.
I shall tell the Führer very clearly,
The fighting in the west must be stopped now;
Every day of war makes things worse for the
German people, victory is out of
The question, I feel responsible to
The German people." He heard that Dollmann,
The Commander of the Seventh Army,
Had died of a "heart attack" when it seemed
The British had broken through his defence.
Rommel drove to Ulm, stayed a night at home,
And then drove on to Berchtesgaden, where,
Exhausted, Rundstedt had arrived, and talked
With loyal Goebbels, treacherous Himmler
And even outspoken Guderian.
At six the conference began, Hitler
Among deferential Generals: Keitel,
And Jodl, later Göring and Dönitz
And air and naval commanders, and Sperrle.
Rommel spoke: "I am here as Commander
Of Heeresgruppe B. It is high time
That, on behalf of the German people
To whom I am answerable, I told
You about the situation in the
West. Now I should like to begin with our
Political situation. The whole
World stands arrayed against Germany, and

This disproportion of strength...." Hitler said,
"Would the brave Field Marshal concern himself
With the military situation,
Not the political one. The front line
In the west must remain where it is, no
Withdrawals. New weapons are coming; new
Fighter planes, more troops." Rommel said, "History
Demands I deal with the *whole* situation.
The Luftwaffe is inadequate, I
Must speak to you about Germany, how
Do you imagine the war can be won?"
Hitler said icily, "Field Marshal, I
Think you had better leave the room." Rommel
Left and travelled back to La Roche Guyon.
That was the last time he would see Hitler.
Hitler summed up: "Because of the Allies'
Superiority in the air and
Naval gunfire, and in mobility,
We must contain them in their bridgehead, then
Drive them back, using mines to interrupt
Supplies, torpedo boats and submarines.
We must fight a war of attrition and
Wear down the enemy like a long siege."
Rommel now stood for a political
Solution to the war, and thus opposed
Hitler's determination to hold ground.

Just as tinder-dry woodlands, set ablaze,
Are beaten down and hosed, and quickly cleared
Wind-breaks, wide paths, stop the advancing fire,
But hot earth carries sparks from root to root
Till, now, a dry gorse bush bursts into flame,
So the Germans beat off the Allied fire
Yet it kept breaking out closer to Caen.
Like a fire-fighter, Rommel beat out flames
Now here, now there, and held the status quo.
Like an arsonist Eisenhower felt rage,
Frustrated at the slowness of his fire,
Impatient for conflagration in Caen.

~ BOOK 2 ~
THE TYRANNICIDES FAIL

O Milton, who at fifty-six years old
Left the plague of London for this Chalfont,
This rural cottage of a regicide,
Fleetwood, found by Thomas Elwood,
And, blind, lived in this study at the back,
Bed near the fireplace, diamond lead windows,
In depression, convinced you had wasted
Twenty years on political pamphlets,
Twenty wasted years given to public life,
For your Paradise to collapse, for all
You stood against with such moral courage
To be restored, which would have cost your life
Had not Clarendon and Marvell saved you;
And, with (like me) a few short poems done,
Having been Cromwell's Latin Secretary
(A Hansard in universal language
To inform all nations of what Cromwell
Had said, almost Foreign Secretary),
And having read all history, literature,
Philosophy and science, and become
A polymath (politician, linguist
Of six languages, mathematician,
Organ-player, singer and gardener),
Who took up the epic you first dreamt of
In Italy and set out in *Mansus*,
And pushed aside for twenty-five long years
(As long as Virgil pushed his task aside)
Except to make a list of cast and notes
Before Cromwell's fine Paradise was lost,
In a workbook before you went blind in
That dreadful year when your wife and son died;
Who, sitting in bed, pacing this wood floor,
Sometimes groping out into the garden,
Waking at four, dictating at noon to
Your wife, daughter or amanuensis,
Sitting, one leg swung over the chair arm,
At perhaps fifty lines a day, finished
Paradise Lost in just over six months
From July sixty-five to January
Sixty-six, shuffling out after "milking"
To eat in the kitchen with your (third) wife,

Elizabeth Minshull, sit on these tiles
Before this fire, or on the brick floor of
This parlour to receive guests; o Milton,
Renaissance man, you who wrote three-quarters
Of your poetic work in the last eight
Years of your life, having reached fifty-six,
As I stand in your study by your quill
And lovingly finger your desk and stools,
I feel your presence and sense its power,
Standing by the fireplace I invoke you,
Sense your encouragement – o blind Milton,
Act as intermediary between
Me and the Muse, help me, send me blank verse
From a source as deep as this well, as sweet
As that green hill, chewed by cows till milking;
Your Satan, like Cromwell, rebelled against
God like a regicide and did not seek
To rule mankind through a New World Order
Like my dark Satan, but inspire me now
I tell of Stauffenberg's rebellion and
The cosmology of Heaven and Hell.

In the geocentric, medieval
Cosmology, invented by Plato,
Aristotle and Ptolemy, and used
By Virgil, Dante, Chaucer, Donne, Shakespeare,
And Milton, though he met Galileo,
Until Newton, the earth, the centre of
The universe, was stationary, ten spheres
Revolved around it, transparent globes filled
With ether, the purest of substances,
For the Moon, Mercury, Venus, Sun, Mars,
Jupiter, Saturn, fixed stars and liquid
Crystalline, hyaline sphere, whose swaying
Explained the equinoctial precessions;
And the Primum Mobile or "first moved",
A hard outer shell, God, the First Mover.
This view of the earth is now out of date:
Uranus, Neptune, Pluto were not known
In this pre-heliocentric model,
And nor were any newer planets that
Spacecraft or Hubble telescope might find,
And so their "sevenfold" earth should be "tenfold"
With thirteen spheres, not ten, around our earth.
Heaven and Hell have both remained the same;

Understandably, despite his physics
Newton changed neither, both have seven spheres,
Which correspond to five geocentric
Planets, the sun and moon, seven bodies,
And from the seventh circle souls can look
At regions more divine or infernal.

Tell, Muse, how Heaven is, and how the veils
Fold round the rose where Christ is found, all love.
In seven rings of increasingly bright Light,
Seven levels, each veiled from the next one,
Each miles wide and merging into the next
So seven seem one as seven ridged fields appear
Part of one landscape, or as on the green
Tiered terraces of Glastonbury Tor
Seven spiralling paths wind up one hill;
There were seven Heavens for departed
Human spirits, and in the empyrean
Above, high Angels shone, Cherubim and
Seraphim, Christ, St. John and St. Bernard,
And beyond them, the great dazzling brilliance
Of the most radiant Light, the Fire, the One.
In the first Heaven or first ring of light,
Behind the veil that hides the Light of God,
Enfolded in bliss, spiritually
Awake, basking in Light, dwell those who have
Glimpsed the Light in their life but who have been
Inconstant to it, like Shelley, Omar
Khayyam or Michelangelo, who have
Pursued other passions though open in
Their intellectual vision, now content
Among the lower Angels who visit
Mankind as messengers. In the second
Heaven, behind another veil, dwell all
Who have opened to the Light in their life
And seen their destiny, the purpose of
Their existence during blissful oneness,
And preserving the view of their senses,
Have become leaders in their active life
Like Cromwell or St. Paul; now full of joy
In the blinding Light. In the third Heaven,
Behind its veil, dwell those who through God's love
Have risen in their life to mysteries
Of creation; who have understood through
Prayer how the universe turns through cycles,

How all is process and growth through the Light,
Like Heracleitus, Plato, Plotinus,
Philosophers who knew the Fire of Love,
Now serene among Principalities.
In the fourth Heaven, behind its veil, dwell
The spiritual Masters, who in their lives
Regularly saw the Light and, being
Teachers, taught it and showed mankind revealed
Wisdom, like the mystic theologians,
Teachers and historians like St. Clement
Of Alexandria, Bonaventure,
Dionysius, Suhrawardi or
Padmasambhava among the Powers. In
The fifth Heaven, behind the veil that hides
It, dwell those who, knowing the blissful Light
Have in their lives approached near the divine,
And praised God from their love of creation,
While having carried forward the Light through war
Like Charlemagne, Bunyan and John Wesley,
Among the Virtuous. In the sixth Heaven,
Behind its veil dwell all the just who have
Been filled with Light and Love from the Most High
And balance mercy and divine justice,
Their vision of what is equitable,
Like Pope Gregory the Great or Cassian,
Filled with righteous peace among Dominions.
In the seventh Heaven, behind the last
Veil dwell, closest to the Great Creator,
All the best contemplatives, who have known
Light in its greatest luminosity,
Pure spirits who in their lives made contact
With the highest Creation, true mystics
Like Sankara, Bayazid, Al-Hallaj,
St. Gregory Palamas, de Léon,
St. Hildegard, Dante, Meister Eckhart,
St. Teresa, St. John of the Cross, Blake,
Julian of Norwich, T. S. Eliot
Among the Thrones.
                    Beyond these seven Heavens
Is the empyrean, where the Light is
Dazzling, where Christ dwells in the centre of
A celestial, sempiternal rose,
Surrounded by saints, Augustine, Bernard,
St. John the Beloved, and the Virgin
Mary, and the coalition leaders,

Founders of minority religions,
Zoroaster, Mahavira, Lao-tzu,
Krishna, the Buddha, Mani, Mohammed,
Hui-neng, Eisai, Dogen, Nanak and Fox,
And Cherubim and Seraphim, a Rose
Of Light whose petals form the scent-like home
Of the Love that invades the universe.
As bees nuzzling in a rose, the Angels
Were honey-gold in the Light of Heaven.

Tell, Muse, how the higher Parliaments work
For both Christ and Satan reacted to
The V-1s, one appalled, one delighted.
Heaven and Hell both have Councils, and both
Look towards earth, which is the battleground
Between them, and provides their policies,
Which are reactions to earthly events,
Attitudes to wars, terrorism, lies.
Heaven has doves and hawks, Hell has meek crows
And vultures. Heaven has conferences
Like the British House of Commons debates,
Where participants have all shades of view
And coalition leaders press their case
And influence the universal Christ
While serving under him, and manoeuvre
To achieve all their political goals.
Hell has speeches, which are made by Satan,
Exhortations, as he harangues his troops
As from a tank, pep talks to raise morale
Like Hitler's addresses at Nuremberg.
And though the high command of Hell obeys
Satan, each has his private view, smiling
To Satan's intense face deceptively.
Satan approves of false appearances,
Deviousness, deception, blatant lies.
In Hell all listen to Satan and say
They agree with him, salute "Hail Satan",
Uniform in their loyalty, their oath
To him which can never be rescinded.
In Heaven mild Christ leads by persuasion,
In Hell ruthless Satan leads by torture
And threats of painful re-execution.

In Heaven, on his rock in a sea of light,
Sombre at the nuclear power Hitler

Threatened when be boasted to boost morale,
Diabolical research to destroy
Angelic man and nature and make him
Overlord of a world like a desert,
Christ stood in his towering light body,
Light far more brilliant than our sun streaming
All round him, so brilliant that earthly eyes
Would be destroyed, only spiritual eyes
Could endure it. All round his body was
A golden halo that became whiteness
Of intense brilliance, and which blended in
To other beings, drew their light to him
In love, as if bright lamps in a large room
Both shone and merged their light in each other;
Only his light was brighter than the rest.
And pressing close, a billion spirits felt
An explosion of unconditional love,
And longed to be embraced, and their knowledge
Remembered him from long before their lives,
Had always known his overflowing joy,
Recalled their missions, what they had to do
To further Being's universal love,
And as questions now came into their minds
Christ's light filled each soul and answers now came
Before they had formed their questions. His light
Filled them with truth and they were one in bliss
As a sea joyfully leaps points of light
In the brilliant sunshine of a spring dawn.
Christ spoke: "You must all understand the point
History has reached, the importance of what
I am about to tell you. It is time.
Differing views of the millennium,
The thousand year kingdom of Christ on earth,
Cite different texts in the scriptures and have
Confused men about my Second Coming.
Pre-, post- and a- (or non-) millennialists
Assert that I will return with my saints
To establish the earthly kingdom that
Was first promised to David in Israel;
That I will return after the Church has
Christianised society; that there will
Be no millennial reign of Christ on earth
Because, as St. Augustine held, the Church
Is my kingdom on earth – just my Second
Coming, and bodily resurrection.

Dispensationalists separate God's
Programmes for Israel and the Church, and say
I will not rule from David's throne within
Jerusalem, but from within the Church
Which began in Fire on Pentecost, and
Pre-tribulationists say my return
Will rapture – come for, save – the entire Church
Before the seven year tribulation and
God's wrath on earth-dwellers, while mid- and post-
Tribulationists say my return will
Fall in the middle or at the end of
The Great Tribulation. All hold that
Armageddon – the battle at Israel's
Har Magedon, which is now on the Plain
Of Megiddo – will end the seven years
Of tribulation and that, once Satan
Is bound in the bottomless pit, then my
Millennial reign of one thousand years
Will begin.
"So who's right? Pre-, post- or a-
Millennialists, dispensationalists,
Or pre-, mid- or post- tribulationists?
Will I return before or after my
Earthly kingdom? Will my Second Coming
Usher in the Eternal State of God?
Know most are partly right! Know that the Church
Is an earthly kingdom among nations,
That Christendom has reigned a thousand years
Through the Holy Roman Empire. Know, too,
Satan was let loose with Napoleon
(By Illuminati, then Bonaparte),
That seven years' tribulation of world war
(Nineteen thirty-nine to forty-five make
An inclusive total of seven years)
Will end in Armageddon from D-Day
To the fall of Berlin, when my return
Must see Israel regathered. Know that while
Satan is bound, nations will start to merge
Into a new order, world government,
So the Church among nations can become
The universal Church of all mankind
And can contain all local religions
Within one Church of Fire or Light, one Whole,
As will be prophesied by our own seer,
Begin a thousand years when all men live

Within a global and eternal state
And can know the metaphysical Light,
Ruled by the Cosmic Christ; as foreseen by
Pre-millennialists, though wider than
Israel, as dispensationalists hold.
The Church among nations is the kingdom,
As a-millennialists say, and my
Return is after this thousand year reign,
As post-millennialists say. Only
The pre-tribulationists are not right;
I go mid-tribulation and do not
Rapture the Church, which does not guard the Light –
Indeed, is a disappointment because
It lost the Light its main role was to guard;
Also post-tribulation, at the end
Of Armageddon. The millennium
Has national and global expressions,
Both earthly and metaphysical forms.
Know it has been, and yet is still to be!
Know of this Universalist kingdom,
Nothing is guaranteed, there is only
Prophecy and our determination.
The Second Coming is to bring it in,
A Church for all mankind, eternal state.
I must now work on earth three or four years,
I must be there till Israel is regathered
And the binding of Satan is begun
By confining him in one area
And then manoeuvring for his downfall."

Puzzled at his mention of the Second
Coming, all listened carefully. Again
Christ spoke: "Now I, an Angel like you all,
The Angel of God, must return to earth
Not to be born in an incarnation,
But to work through our new emanation,
Be with supporters such as Bonhoeffer.
Beloved John will accompany me.
He saw Nero Redivivus as Beast
(Apollyon was Apollo Nero);
There was a legend Nero did not die
But escaped to Parthia, whence he planned
To return to Rome. In fact John's timing
Was out, the threat was the barbarian
Invasions. Through Charlemagne I set up

My Church's earthly kingdom in the west,
My millennium there when we were still
In time of nations, the Holy Roman
Empire. After that the Antichrist ruled
As John prophesied, and persecution
Worse than Nero's – millions are being killed –
Is with us now, though not in Israel's land
But among the Jews of Europe. Hitler
Must be defeated, I must see to that.
John's Armageddon is in Normandy,
For that is where the Germans must retreat
And Satan and his dark powers withdraw.
Through our beloved Constantine the Great
I founded a thousand year old empire
In the east, the Byzantine, which became
Russian Orthodox and was taken by
Satan through his Communist stooge Lenin.
My splendid western thousand year empire,
The Holy Roman Empire, was also
Taken by Satan, through his dark agent
Hitler, who has now declared his own vile
Millennium which imitates our two,
His thousand year Third Reich, which he claims will
Commence the rule of Heaven after this
Armageddon – yet is the rule of Hell
As Satan has stolen a march on us
And is trying to seize what prophecy
Has foretold is our destiny, and seeks
To establish our millennium as
A tyranny that shelters every vice.
We must defeat Satan's millennium.
John foretold that I would conquer Satan
At the end of time, that the Day of Judgement
Would then follow. Both Axis and Allies
Are working on a new, awesome weapon
Which can destroy the earth and wipe out man,
Destroy the creation of the Most High
And so end time, for on the earth no minds,
No consciousness would be aware of time,
There would only be our eternity.
Satan wants this new weapon to destroy
The earth, man and creation, and end time,
And I must return to preserve them all,
Earth, man, creation, time, and crush Satan,
Slow the evil research, speed up the good

And wrest the new weapon from evil hands,
Deliver it to good for safekeeping.
The final battle between Light and Darkness
Is being fought in Normandy and here
As Michael prepares to invade Chaos
And capture Satan. Hitler, Antichrist,
Threatens to destroy the three rulers in
London, Washington, Moscow with this new
Terrible weapon, make Satan supreme.
Fellow Angels, the end of time must be
On our terms, not Satan's; I must assist
The Allies by returning to earth now
And set in motion the lengthy process
Which will result in universal peace
For all the learning spirits on the earth.
Nothing is guaranteed; the outcome will
Follow from our efforts and influence."
He spoke, and when he had ended, there was
A silence, as, stunned by sadness, all grasped
That they would lose their leader for a while.
They all hummed a music, angelic sound
Of great sweetness, mellifluous assent.

Christ spoke again: "We are against killing
In all forms, including killing in war,
But Satan's influence has extended
And there is killing on a massive scale.
Among the Jews it is now systematic:
Since the Wannsee conference, eight million
European Jews have become targets
For extermination, even Jews in
Ireland and Albania. Each day souls pour
Like refugees to Heaven. One man is more
Responsible for this than all others
And he is raining V-1s on London
And trying to build an atomic bomb
That will be used against the three Allies.
He is in Satan's camp, despite the prayers
Of millions we receive daily we have
Little influence with Hitler, and so
We are forced to face the question: is it
Better for mankind that he should die now?
Clearly the answer's Yes. There is a plot
To kill him which seems to have a good chance
Of success. We are forced to ask: is it

Better for mankind that the plot should work?
And should we support it? If the answer
To the first question is Yes, I submit
The answer to the second must be Yes
Too. We must support killing for the prize:
The end of the war, the saving of lives.
Twenty-five million have already died
In the five years of war so far; at least,
As Hitler's Barbarossa invasion
May have killed forty million Russians, and
Fifteen million Chinese have died; and I
Estimate thirty million more will die
(Three times the deaths in the Great War, and far
More than Napoleon's dead, or previous wars')
Unless *he* dies. And if he dies we will
Have prevented a wicked, murderous use
Of the atomic bomb. In this one case
Ends justify the means. The alternative
Is worse, that Hitler lives and millions more
Should die, and tracts of Europe and elsewhere
Should be a desert. It is either-or.
We have always held in Heaven that we,
Who are against killing, cannot allow
Someone to kill on a colossal scale,
And so we must condone killing one man
To oppose his killing thirty million.
Tyrannicide advances the world's good.
I must keep the universe in order.
Satan must not be allowed power over
Atomic warfare, indiscriminate
Power to devastate the earth and mankind.
In Heaven we can only love, the Light force
Cannot kill. That power has been granted to
The dark force of destruction, of Satan.
Only men and demons can kill. We can
Only suggest. And my conscience is now
Troubled, for though we act from Love,
We must encourage Stauffenberg, who is
Leading the conspirators, to act in
A Hellish way. But as his aim is just
He will eventually join us here
And not find himself in another place.
As to encourage him, though Love, seems Hate,
I will not delegate this task to such
As Michael, but will perform it myself

So that Love does not blur to destruction.
I take full responsibility for
This act, which lies at the margin of our
Powers. Therefore, to sum up this tangled plan,
I propose that we support the bomb plot
To kill Hitler, and that I should approach
Heisenberg, who saw our latent order
As random and uncertain, and persuade
Him to slow down the atomic programme,
Using deception to outdeceive lies
And to secure the triumph of the truth,
In full knowledge that to govern a flawed
Universe requires us to face and cope
With moral conundrums, as much as man."

Tell, Muse, how Hell appears, and how the veils
Fold round the thorn where Satan hangs, the Lie.
In seven rings of increasingly dim dark,
Seven Hells lurk like dark descending caves
To which all souls are drawn by the degree
Of shadow or darkness in their nature,
Seven levels, each veiled from the last one,
Each miles wide and merging into the next
So seven seem one, as seven caves appear
Part of one long cavern in Wookey Hole –
Through which, underground, flows the River Axe
Whose million-year old swirl has carved chambers
Where clear green pools lie under stalactites –
When seen from the path that leads down into
The fissured limestone walls of the last cave.
Beyond a dark wood and a vestibule
Where slump, heads bowed, the souls of the futile,
Who, rejecting and rejected, wait, bored;
In the first Hell, in gloom, among horseshoe
And pipistrelle bats hanging from the roof,
Dwell those who can be rescued, virtuous
Heretics with rational-social outlooks,
Who were proud with a high opinion of
Their merits, exalted and arrogant,
Novelists, dramatists and poetasters,
Rationalists and humanists, scholars,
Positivist philosophers, their dupes,
And reductionist scientists, and theirs,
And sceptical materialists, who,
Though agnostic or atheist and not

Aware of the Light have lead blameless lives –
Democritus, Newton, Darwin and Freud –
With souls of pallid greyness, along with
School inspectors, teachers, doctors, dentists,
Police and all who ran the State system,
Insurers, traffic wardens, the blameless
Church-goers who sang hymns and said rote prayers
And missed the Light, the essence of all faiths,
Because the vicar was not mystical,
And here dwell many vicars in this murk,
Archbishops, Cardinals, ministers, priests,
Who recited mechanical prayers from
A book, and missed the vision of the Light.
Here each endlessly proclaimed his creed and
Knowing it was wrong, felt dissatisfied.
In the second Hell, in darker torment,
Dwell in dampness the lustful, all who have
Been attached to their sensual desires,
Slaves to the need for gratification
Rather than masters of their deep passions,
All who had self-indulgent appetites –
Messalina, Casanova, Harris –
The incontinent who lacked discipline,
A ring of whores and Don Juans, whose itch
Or ache kept them in body consciousness,
Which used others as objects, instruments,
So their souls were never lit by a ray
Of Light and never grew. And also here
Were lovers and mistresses whose desires
Distracted them from truth during their lives,
Who broke up others' unions, brought grief
To others and deprived them of the Light,
Government Ministers, Princes and Kings,
Nobility and workers side by side,
Their souls unreachable like nuts in shells;
Here they itch, twitch and ache without relief.
In the third Hell, in still dingier gloom,
Dwell the gluttonous, all who preferred food
And drinking and loud laughter in taverns
To contemplation which opens the soul
To the Light and starts its growth, like a shoot,
All who surrendered to their appetites –
Lucullus, Henry the Eighth, De Quincey –
A ring of social hostesses and guests
Addicted to alcohol, nicotine,

Drugs and time-wasting, passing many hours
In hazy consciousness, an illusion
Of togetherness: here hunger and thirst
Torment them in their perpetual fast.
In the fourth Hell, in even darker murk,
Dwell the hoarders and spendthrifts, all who had
A selfish appetite for money, and
Were avaricious, greedy for their gain,
Were misers or extravagant spenders –
Midas, Rothschilds, Rockefellers and Ford –
Attached to their greed, too busy earning
Fortunes or shopping, using merchandise,
Cars, computers, lazy sun-holidays –
Profiteers, property developers,
Bankers, stockbrokers and solicitors,
Stock exchange players and estate agents,
Lawyers, accountants and tax inspectors –
To contemplate and open to the Light
And journey up the Mystic Way, progress,
Their acquisitive consciousness having
Barred them from growing their souls; here, endless
Craving to hoard or spend, unsatisfied,
Leaves them in permanent numb frustration.
In the fifth Hell deeper in darkness and
Egocentricity and selfishness,
Dwell the wrathful, all who have assaulted
Or attacked others in fits of anger,
Who did not learn to control their temper,
Disputed heatedly, felt bitterness,
Felt scorn and yearned for revenge, and believed –
William Conqueror, Philip the Second –
Humiliation must be answered, who
Were quick to take offence, so did not seek
Quiet or meditate to bring in the calm
The Light gives, serenity and peace that
Passeth understanding, political
Agitators, demonstrators, MPs,
Football crowds and players, beer-drinkers and
Revolutionaries whose consciousness
Was too much on society or men
To be transformed by Light; here, endlessly
Stirred to rage by no cause, and unable
To express it, they boil and seethe within,
Simmer as if insulted, discontent.

In the sixth Hell, in deepening darkness
And self-assertion, caring for no one
But themselves, as if locked in a dungeon,
Envying the good fortune of others,
Resenting and coveting beauty, wealth,
Dwell the violent, all who have struck a blow
Against their neighbours, robbers, murderers
Who have injured fellow human beings
By theft or bestial bodily assault –
De Sade, Dick Turpin and Jack the Ripper –
And the fraudulent who out of malice
Have tricked their neighbours, cheated or swindled
Them of their earned savings, being attached
To advancing their own interests and not
Opening to the Light's gentle calm and
Loving their neighbour in the unified
Vision, violently separating
Themselves from the Light's truth; here too are found
The tyrants who had tens of thousands killed,
Who could not complete their divine mission –
Robespierre, Napoleon, Lenin and Haig –
And suicides, who out of self-hatred
Ended their own lives, ignoring the Light
Which reveals to all men their destiny,
And all who have been violent towards God,
Nature and art, who have gouged out the earth
Or damaged paintings, both God's creation;
Polluters and wilful hewers of trees.
Here an endless desire to harm fills all,
But they cannot express it and so feel
Frustrated, murderous and unhappy.
In the seventh Hell, in night darkness dwell
The spiritually slothful, the most
Ignorant who deceived their neighbours, who
Were not misguided but deliberate,
Fraudsters who falsified reality,
Who corrupted and perverted others,
Panders, pimps, seducers who degraded,
Flatterers who exploited rank desires,
All who made money out of the pure Light,
All fortune-tellers who used psychic powers
And magic to foretell the future known
Only to the Light and who stole money
Out of public office, betraying trust,

All hypocrites who misled others' souls,
All thieves who stole from others, all who
Advised others to practise fraud and sowed
Discord in religion, town, family,
All falsifiers of accounts, and all
Who were brutal with a deceiving smile,
Who authorised foul genocide, all who
Were separate from mankind, practised Satan's
Deceit and so are closest to Satan,
To the Lie which would falsify all truth –
Cagliostro, Marx, Illuminati –
And farthest from opening to the Light,
Their attention on corrupting others.
Here a perpetual yearning to gull
Others fills their minds without expression,
And their craving to chat is unfulfilled
And leaves them endlessly discontented
And miserable. In all seven Hells
One glimpse of Light can take a spirit out
Of Hell and put it in the first Heaven;
As in the dark regions of Hell no light
Penetrates, redemption by Light cannot
Be expected.
Beyond these seven Hells
Is pitch darkness of chaos, where light is
Absent, where Satan dwells in the centre
Of a thorn, guarded by prickles, hanging
Like a bat (as his form Odin hung on
The World Tree), near a cesspit where all waste
Matter decays before, recycled, it
Flows back into existence; surrounded
By Arch-demons, forms his emanation
Spawned in fornications, incarnations
Both aliases of himself and children,
Such as Baal, Sammael, Beliar, Abaddon,
His Hindu-like manifestations as
Idol, seducer, fornicator and
Destroyer; and by all his disciples,
Simon Magus, Roderic Borgia (Pope
Alexander the Sixth), Adam Weishaupt,
Eliphas Levi, Aleister Crowley,
Rasputin; in a thicket of Darkness
Whence, like the Axe through underground caverns,
Decomposed, broken down into new forms,
Its force and consciousness again released,

Matter flows out into the universe,
Polluted with deception and falsehood.

Then, disguised as Lucifer, dazzling with
False light that filled with wonder the dark things
Of Hell, near-blinding them with promise of
The Heavenly destiny they had missed,
Like a sun in the thick darkness of Hell,
Sly Satan, the cunning black shadow, spoke:
"Angels, shades of darkness, powers that are free!
By our own efforts we have managed things
So that we have our own millennium;
We have shown Christ that *we* should run *our* earth
Through our thousand year Third Reich. Christ may have
More representatives in his unfair
Parliament, but we have shown where power is.
We must defend our millennium, which
Our great Hitler set up on our behalf,
From the deceitful bandit Christ. Angels,
Our spies have learned of a plot to kill our
Hitler. Urged on by our enemy, false,
Perfidious Christ, the German Army
Plans to place a bomb near our great leader.
We will prevent that. But our spies have learned
More, that Christ himself is leaving Heaven
To perpetrate this foul act. Angels, this
Is our opportunity, we can strike
In his absence, we can invade Heaven
When it is leaderless. We need to make
A diversion, to keep Christ occupied
While we wrest Heaven from him, and I know
What we should do. Stalin, he is the key.
We have had contacts with Stalin, he is
Already a friend of ours, we approve
Of all he has done, we contrived that he
Should form an alliance with our Hitler,
And we supported our Hitler when he
Launched Barbarossa against Stalin's might
As this was necessary for our plan.
It was expedient to attack Moscow.
We have supported both sides since Stalin
Began to drive the Germans back, we have
Renewed our championship of Stalin's cause.
I will recruit Stalin to our side, I
Will encourage his natural bent to lie,

To deceive his Allies, further his ends –
And ours too. I will sow dissension in
The treacherous Allies, create great doubt
Between Stalin and the rest of them, and
They will not know that we are behind it.
We will then have both Hitler and Stalin,
The mighty German Empire and the vast
Tracts of the Soviet Union – both sides!
This, all along, has been my secret plan.
Buzz if you think this is a good idea."
There was a roar of buzzing, all approved.
Satan strutted, proud and narcissistic,
Like a pop star in a glittering coat,
Head back in demoniac energy,
Raising his hands for applause, basking in
Admiration, preening himself, full of
Self-love, over-desirous to impress.

Now, surrounded by his Arch-demons Baal,
Sammael, Beliar, Abaddon, Satan-
Lucifer spoke again to the great throng
Of sycophants and flatterers who fed
His self-esteem and overweening pride,
Devious, ahead of the situation,
Creating mischief from which his cause could
Profit, seeking to deceive, plausible
Not specific, like a politician:
"We want the Russian offensive to make
Christ's advisers alarmed. We want a drive
Towards Berlin, so they doubt good Stalin's
Intentions. We want him to lie.
We need to strengthen Stalin's thrust towards
Our ally Hitler, to confuse mankind,
We need to spread our ideas, so man trusts
Us. We have already found on all sides
Acceptance of our greater strategy,
For through the diversion of Stalin, which
Will tie Christ up in knots, many men will
Side with Stalin against Hitler, and fall
Under our power, see Communism as
Good and fail to see our workings, and when
We can twist man into a new belief
He thinks is good, without recognising
Our own involvement, then we have got him!
Angels, be alert to the ultimate

Aim of my plan, what we will do to man.
Even more than to rule Heaven, I want
To be worshipped as God by all mankind –
And this will empower you, my followers –
For then I will enslave mankind and take
My true place as Lord of the Universe.
We have succeeded in persuading man
That I do not exist, that I am but
A freak instance of behaviour that is
Inhumane or anti-social, a quirk
Or kink in the minds of men that can be
Called psychological. We have also
Tried to convince men that evil is good,
To make them feel comfortable as they
Do our will. To many I am only
A metaphor. We want them to go on
Thinking that way. To many evil is
Mere absence of good; our victims before
The killing wall know better. Many, too,
Attribute their ills to us, when we can
Merely persuade their hearts and minds with lies
And illusions; we cannot compel men.
We are implacably opposed to Truth
For Truth is of God and the divine plan,
Which we again oppose. God wants the earth
To evolve to consciousness filled with Light,
God wants all men to be illumined and
To walk in enlightened serenity.
We want all mankind to be restless and
Discontented, and ill-disposed to God.
Illusion draws men to us. God wants all
Mankind to evolve as Angels of Light.
Our plan sees men as demons of Darkness."
So Lucifer spoke, brilliant in dark Hell
With meretricious light that seemed of Heaven,
And that deceived his yearning listeners.
And like a wrestler in a world-class ring
Who listens, hand to ear, on all four sides
And hears the rapturous tumult, applause,
And who handclaps to orchestrate the roar
Of public support and adoration –
So Satan preened himself before the throng,
So Satan led the crowd's adulation.

Churchill, in the Cabinet War rooms, stared

At a telegram from Switzerland, which
The Foreign Office had copied. It said
Eight hundred thousand Hungarian Jews
Had been deported to Birkenau, near
Oswiecim, where a million and a half
Jews had already been killed. Appalled, he
Wrote to Eden, "What can be done?", then stared,
Trying to comprehend a death camp where
Systematic killing took place. News of
The horror had been brought by escapers
And air photos, but only now did he
Grasp that Hitler meant to erase all trace
Of the race and line of eight million Jews.
He wrote to Eden, "There is no doubt that
This is probably the greatest and most
Horrible single crime ever commit-
-ted in the whole history of the world."

Descending from the clouds, invisible,
Like a sky-diver in free fall, at speed,
Christ saw a dismal work of fallen man,
A Hell on earth where Satan's tortures ruled.
At Birkenau, a train drew up, hundreds
Of Jews in coats, hats and head-scarves climbed out
Of closed waggons and lined up on the ramp,
To await selection. Men who could work
Trudged through the gate under the tower till they
Came to a gate above which was inscribed
"Arbeit Macht Frei", work makes one free, a lie.
Women and children tramped towards a wood
And queued near doors which were labelled "Showers".
Powerless to alter things, Christ floated on.

Eisenhower sent John back to Washington
With Kay in his B17 Flying
Fortress. At the airport Ike's wife Mamie
Greeted them pleasantly, then left with John
Who invited Kay for drinks the next day.
Kay was in uniform among summer
Dresses. Mamie scrutinised her and when
John said he was taking Kay to New York
To see *Oklahoma!* she pulled a face
And said, "I'm sure Miss Summersby does not
Want to go to New York in all this heat."
Kay, sensing Mamie's disapproval, urged

John to cancel the plan, but he had seen
What Kay meant to his father, and they went,
Despite gossip in Washington about
The glamorous driver the General used
Kay felt on display and longed for England.

Dismayed at the slow gains of the British
Round Caen, and irritated by the claims
That slowness was a feature of the plan,
Impatient to escape the flying bombs
Whose launch sites Montgomery should capture,
Bold Eisenhower, openly speaking of
Cautious Montgomery's failure at Caen,
Flew to Normandy to accelerate
Operations. He took a bedroll and
Two men, and for five days, visited troops
And battle zones, and talked with commanders
Who had to guard him from occasional
Artillery fire. Next Sunday morning
With Bradley he drove to Montgomery
At Blay, and, waiting for him to return,
Eisenhower wandered slowly on his own.

Eisenhower's stroll took him to the open
Hillside in meadows of a farm. He gazed
At a pond where blue-needle dragonflies
Hovered like heavy bombers near a frog.
He saw azure harebells hang in couchgrass,
And as he wandered, alone, corn-cockle
And cornflower in a wheatfield, a rabbit,
A magpie moth flitted, a finch flew by,
A turtle dove cooed. He found a cottage
Covered in wild clematis, saw wood-witch
Fungus and ferns and found a glow-worm, which
He held in his hand. It resembled an
Armour-plated car. A swallow swooped, he
Watched a worm and a snail, and rejoiced in
Little slithering things in the warm sun,
A lizard, an adder. He felt alive,
Removed from war in peaceful farmland where
Nature was content to flit, droop and slide.
Here Christ found him and stood invisible,
And poured in reassuring thoughts about
Montgomery, for he knew what was in
The troubled heart of this now peaceful man

Who escaped responsibility by
Gazing at small things ignorant of war.

At length, Montgomery arrived from church
In black beret, sweater and corduroys,
Two puppies playing near two captured tanks,
And took the men to his map caravan
And briefed them on his strategy, which was
To contain German armour round Caen while
General Bradley broke out from near Cherbourg.
Eisenhower was stunned by the clarity
And logic of his plan, and by his self-
Belief, his conviction, his charisma,
Professionalism and physical
Presence. He did not mention Anvil and
Came out saying, "This bocage is not tank
Country, I can see you can't go faster."
While he was in Montgomery's presence
Eisenhower was under his spell, but when
He was back in England he thought him slow
And was influenced by carping comments,
As when Tedder and Smith told him the blame
For slowness lay with Montgomery, not
The air force. In a letter Eisenhower
Set out his objectives, but did not press
Montgomery to implement action.

Eisenhower was working in Bushey Park
Headquarters the next Saturday when his
Office door opened and Kay entered. He
Grinned, rose and put his arms round her, breathing,
"I'm so glad you're back." That evening they sat
In the garden at Telegraph Cottage
Until the sunset had faded, sipping
Champagne while pleased Eisenhower squeezed Kay's
hand.
They chattered in the twilight without strain,
Sharing experiences till a buzz-
Bomb drove them into the shelter. A few
Days later they again sat out, watching
Their black dog Telek roll on his back, paws
In the air, and Kay said, "It's like having
A child come home after he's been away
At school for the first time," and Eisenhower
Said quietly, "Would you like to have a child?"

Kay said, "Yes, I'd love to have a baby,
Not *a* baby, *your* baby. But it is
Impossible." Eisenhower sighed, "I know,
But maybe things will be different later.
I'd like it. I'd like it very much." They
Sat in silence, and each time their eyes met
A new level of intimacy called.
Flying bombs whined, they slept in the shelter
And Eisenhower reached out into the dark
And they fell asleep holding hands between
Their cots like two young teenagers in love,
Chaste save for the hand contact they allowed,
Yet with bodies aching for each other
As if they slept in a tent in a wood,
Safe from the distant whine of mosquitoes.

Hitler was displeased that his Generals
Rommel and Rundstedt both wished to withdraw
Behind the Seine. When Epsom broke, shaken,
Rommel's commander of the Seventh Army,
Dollmann poisoned himself at his HQ,
And his commander of Panzer Group West,
Von Schweppenburg, wished to retreat from Caen.
Rundstedt agreed and sent his report to
Armed Forces HQ. On the telephone
Keitel asked plaintively, "What shall we do?"
"What shall we do?" Rundstedt replied. "Make peace,
You fools!" Informed, next day Hitler retired
Him on the grounds of age and health, replaced
Him with von Kluge, a specialist in
Defence against armoured breakthroughs, while he
Dismissed Schweppenburg for defeatism.
Rommel was now the only member of
The German high command in Normandy
To survive from D-Day, and he believed
The unequal struggle was near its end.

On the anniversary of Heinrich
The First, the Fowler's, death, Himmler went off
To the Romanesque crypt in Quedlinburg
And at his tomb communed with his spirit
As it was then, which he had come to think
Had now reincarnated in himself,
Summoned it back across a thousand years,
And received advice from a German King

Of the Saxon dynasty who conquered
The Slavs, and who epitomised Himmler's
Hatred of the Poles, Slavs he would suppress.

Now he had failed to secure the Orne line
Montgomery had no choice but to mount
A frontal assault on Caen. Eisenhower
Heard that Canadians attacked all day
And took part of Le Carpiquet village.
Some ended where they started, with wounded.
Heavy bombers bombed Caen and raised morale,
But missed the outlying German strongpoints.
At dawn the British and Canadians
Attacked Caen in Operation Charnwood.
In a day of fierce and bloody fighting
The Allies prised the Germans from north Caen
With casualties more severe than D-Day's.
German armour and artillery came
To defend south and east Caen, and secure
Hill 112. Bradley tried to break out
Of the bocage along a broad front line.
Dempsey sought to drive east of Caen across
Open country, and with heavy bombers
Destroy the German front-line troops. Cautious
Montgomery, however, modified
The plan. At dawn Allied bombers dropped flares
And then bombed the German positions for
Two hours. Many German troops were killed or
Wounded, Tiger tanks blown into the air
Like leaves in an autumn gale. Germans came
Out of foxholes to surrender. Elsewhere
Sherman tanks went up in flames, ambushed by
German tanks and anti-tank guns hidden
In villages. Caen was cleared, Bourguébus
Village secured, a seven-mile advance
To the ridge cost four hundred tanks and five
Thousand men. Meanwhile the Americans
Thrust into the hill country and hedgerows
In a heat haze. The Germans drove them off
With thousands of artillery shells, and
The Americans lost a thousand men
Trying to take the hill above St. Lô.
After relieving a trapped battalion
Major Howie was killed by a German
Shell. A task force entered St. Lô, bringing

On a jeep Howie's body, which they lay
On the steps of the ruined church draped in
An American flag, and all who passed
Bowed their heads to one who had shown the way
Out of the hedgerows and of Normandy.

In Berlin's Institute for Physics met
On July the twelfth, with Heisenberg as
Host, serving fresh raspberries, milk and wine,
For once not in his lab in Hechingen,
The Wednesday Club, whose learned talks, dinner
And convivial conversation masked
A plot to overthrow Hitler. Here Beck,
Popitz, Schulenberg, Goerdeler and more
Heard Heisenberg talk on nuclear fission,
Which Otto Hahn discovered in Berlin.
Beck said, "If atomic energy could
Be used for bombs, all military ideas
Would have to be changed." Heisenberg had felt
No atom bombs could be built till the war
Was over, as he had told Seyss-Inquart,
A local German ruler in Holland
Who had said, "If you can develop this
Super weapon, the Allies may give up
Their air raids and rely on their armies
And lose the war." Hans Frank, the Governor-
General of Poland, had also urged
Him to develop the atomic bomb,
As had Himmler, chief of the Gestapo.
Beck, who would be Head of State when Hitler
Had fallen, said no more. When all had gone,
Heisenberg stood in the dark garden near
The raspberry canes, and recalled how he had
Met Bohr in Copenhagen to discuss
"The moral issues", but in fact prevent
The atomic bomb from being made worldwide,
And how he disclosed the existence of
The German bomb programme, with clearance from
Weizsäcker, Wirtz, Jensen and Houtermans,
And said to Bohr, "We know that we can make
Atomic bombs," which shocked him, and, "We should
Not even attempt to work on such bombs."
Dazed, Bohr had said, "It's inevitable
That in wartime all physicists should work
For their own governments, that's justified."

Heisenberg had wanted all physicists
To band together in opposition
To their governments and the atomic bomb.
And now, under pressure from Himmler and
Urged on by Beck, he stared into the dark,
Musing, and was startled to hear a voice
Speak in German with quiet authority:
"Werner, you are right. What is in your heart
Is right. Do not make an atomic bomb."
He looked, and by a raspberry cane discerned
A faintly glowing form with a kind face
He instantly knew. Incredulously
He murmured, "Is it you?" With infinite
Compassion, the shape said, "Yes. You are right.
It would be disastrous if Hitler had
Just one atomic bomb. Many want you
To make sure this does not happen. Go slow
In your research, do not listen to Beck.
Carry your team with you. Consider this,
Germany discovered nuclear fission,
Controls Europe's only uranium
Mines, and the world's only heavy-water
Plant in Norway, and has you, who are now
The world's greatest practising physicist,
Having invented quantum mechanics
By formulating atomic systems
In terms of matrices, having stated
Your new uncertainty principle and
Revolutionised theoretical
Physics – not believing with Einstein that
All is in fundamental harmony,
As I can assure you it is, as you
Will one day come to see, when you are dead
(Though you are right that the observation
Of Positivists is theory-laden);
You, who will not desert your country, you
Who will remain in Germany, so your
Brainpower can win the war for Hitler by
Making an atomic bomb, as you half
Want to do." Stunned by the shape's deep knowledge,
Heisenberg breathed "You know me well." The shape
Continued: "The Germans had six months' start
Over the Americans, or a year
Even. How you have thought is right, but you
Must not weaken. You want Beck to destroy

Hitler, but you want Germany to win
The war. Do not make an atomic bomb
So Germany can win this hideous war,
So Hitler can wrest victory from defeat.
Do not be tempted." Heisenberg put in,
"The Americans threaten to destroy
Dresden with an atomic bomb, unless
Germany surrenders." The shape said, "I
Promise you, no atomic bomb will drop
On Dresden. Enough, I have said enough.
You know what we expect, do what is right
You must sacrifice the chance of a world
Reputation, fame greater than you have,
Which is worthless beside two billion lives,
The sum total of mankind in this year.
Do what is right and save man from the worst
Disaster – catastrophe – ever known.
And you will not tell anyone about
My visit to you, and if you do, they
Will say you had a hallucination,
A waking dream." Heisenberg said, "I can
Falsify the maths to prevent German
Science from developing the atom
Bomb." A deception worthy of Satan!
The shape smiled and faded like a thin mist.
Heisenberg called to him, imploring him
To stay, but the shape faded before he
Could be questioned about the random's place
In a harmonious universe run
By the mist-like form with a caring face.
Heisenberg rubbed his eyes, knew it was real.

The German high command in the Wehrmacht,
Including Kluge and many Generals,
Were dismayed at their Commander-in-Chief,
Hitler.'s plans for conquest. They doubted that
They could defeat the vast Soviet army,
Saw danger from the east, dreaded Soviet
Occupation, hoping to ally with
The Western Allies, America and
Britain, against the ruthless east. Plans were
Made to assassinate Hitler, arrest
The main Nazis, and under Rommel if
He could be persuaded, or Ludwig Beck,
Once Army Chief of Staff, negotiate

Peace with the Western Allies which would save
Germany from occupation, and form
An anti-Soviet front. The man chosen
To carry out the killing, Count Claus von
Stauffenberg, had one arm and only three
Fingers on his one hand, after being
Machine-gunned near Sfax. In hospital he
Recovered from bullet wounds to his eyes,
Right forearm and hand, which were shot away,
And shrapnel in his legs, one knee and back,
And felt he had survived for a reason,
To fulfil a purpose, to save the Reich
And redeem the honour of Germany.
Count Stauffenberg's magnificent presence,
Force and soldier's record made him first choice
To co-ordinate and perform the deed
He thought and spoke of as tyrannicide
Though being a one-armed and one-eyed man.
When Hitler stared, forcing all eyes aside,
Ruling them with the sheer force of his will,
Hypnotising them by his magic arts,
Stauffenberg had outstared him in Ukraine.
He could have presided over the new
Provisional government but, shunning
All positions of personal power,
He was content with Under-Secretary
Of State for War, a modest role for one
Who had been first mover of the idea.
He had become Chief of Staff to Fromm, the
Commander-in-Chief of the Home Army,
From July the first, and could operate
His coup as an order by Fromm to troops
To secure the country while the Army
Arrested all Nazis and seized power.
He had access to Hitler, Himmler and
Göring. He was prepared to kill Hitler
On July the eleventh at the Berghof
But he had aborted his plan. Having
Observed how near he'd come, and overheard
The plotters, both Christ and Satan watched him.

There is a view that God knows no evil,
For if he did, infinite mind and love
Would contain evil; that if God knew sin
He would be a sinner; that evil is

Not real but is created by man, and
Is the mere absence of good; that God tempts
No man, being pure, and that, becoming
The infinite mind, man thinks only good;
That Satan is only an idea in
Man's foolish mind. Such a view is not right.
God contains all, and thus includes evil,
Uses it to further his purposes,
The cosmic power of darkness, formerly
Of Ahriman, then Lucifer, and now
Cosmic Satan, deception, illusion
And lie, who acts as God's agent without
Realising it, for God's purposes
Require men to deceive and seem and lie.
Man cannot choose good till he knows evil.
Satan's temptations have a moral force
Because they have moral consequences.
Just as the Cosmic Christ channels truth, light
And life, so the Cosmic Satan channels
The lie, darkness and death. Both opposites,
Both moral forces are parts of the whole,
Both manifested from the latent One,
And the world is their battleground. They meet
In the universe and compete on earth,
For both camps seek to win man to their view
And in the struggle of conflicting choice
Man transcends himself and achieves greatness,
Defining himself by his opposite,
Choosing the good against evil each day,
Right against wrong, truth against lie, and light
Against dark. Satan is real, look where he
Deceives. Satan shapes man by providing
Conditions his spirit can rise above,
Deceptions, illusions and lies that give
Nobility to his immortal soul,
When overcome. Without realising it
Satan performs a necessary work
Within the greater will of Knowing God
And helps bring in the true millennium,
The thousand year long universal Church.

Tell, Muse, how such a universe is Love,
How Christ walked the earth radiating Love.
The Cosmic Christ is the divine "I am",
The pattern that connects all atoms and
Galaxies of the universe in Love,

For it is Love that moves the universe,
Not accident as reductionists think,
And gives it order, so, seen as a whole,
It is a cosmos, ordered by the Light,
Not processes of atoms running down.
In vain stargazers peer for cosmic Love.
The universe, according to small stars
Around the Milky Way, is now sixteen
Billion years old; and yet the Hubble Space
Telescope shows M100 in Virgo
Is receding faster, and from nearer,
Than previously thought, and is some eight
To twelve billion years old. The universe
Cannot be four billion years younger than
Some objects in it: either it does not
Expand so fast; or the stars are younger;
Or, as the universe began to swell
Its expansion has accelerated.
Tell, Muse, how Einstein's cosmological
Constant holds that the universe used to
Expand more slowly, through a repulsive
Force which balanced the attraction of all
Matter and kept the universe static.
This is the expanding force of the Fire
That counteracts the force of gravity
And gives all particles a vast, stable
Interconnectedness – the force Hubble
Found. This force that makes the universe swell
Like a balloon is Love, the Cosmic Christ,
The Fire that orders things to its purpose,
Which is governed by the Eternal Light.

Tell, Muse, how evil grew out of the Fire,
How tyranny grew out of Unity,
How genocide grew out of One, the Light,
How Hate grew out of Love. First all was Fire,
Potential Fire in divine darkness, then
More defined Darkness grew from which came Light,
And dark Ignorance grew out of Knowledge.
When the Angels fell they had sparks of Light
Which they denied, living in Delusion
And Self-Deception, and moved out from Fire
Into darkness, absence of Fire or Light,
Voluntarily and rebelliously
Depriving themselves of their birthright spark,

Eschewing positive for negative
Energy, wilfully living error,
Allying with the Darkness, connecting
With its power, which came out of the Fire to
Be one of two forces that shaped matter;
Allying with Satan, who had a role
In creating the universe for God.
The Cosmic Satan's force is Ignorance,
Delusion, Deception. Its ambition
To rule mankind performs God's will as a
Necessary Destroyer, for all things
That are created must, by destruction,
Return to the source to be recycled.
Satan is God's grimed recycling dustman,
Disposer of waste like a sewage firm.
Satan's power of Darkness is a vital
And necessary function that maintains
The efficient running of God's bright world.
Satan is motivated by belief
That he will one day rule Heaven, and so
His destructive and demoniac power
Encroaches everywhere as God would wish,
And humans like Eckart and Hitler can
Tap into it, in the illusion that
It is the power of God, of the white Light.
Eckart and Hitler were grossly deceived
(If they did not deliberately distort)
In labelling this Darkness Ahura
And their main foe Jehovah-Ahriman.
In fact their power was Darkness, Ahriman,
And in their Ignorance they stood against
The light of Ahura Mazda and Christ,
In their Delusion, deceived by Satan,
They thought the Antichrist was the divine.
Their evil mixed Ignorance and a Power.

As the macrocosm so also the
Microcosm of the subtle body
Where inner centres take in occult power.
It too has two forces that move through it,
One contracting force of seven or more wheels
Or chakras that take energy in and
Implode it into the subtle body
As in Tantric Hindu Kundalini;
And one expanding force of some ten gates

In the Taoist scheme that rotates all
Energy received and explodes it out
From the subtle body as inner Light,
Mysterious secret of the Golden Flower.
Compare the Kabbalistic sephiroth,
Ten centres which receive from the beyond
And manifest it in four separate worlds;
Compare the Christian subtle body where
The heart centre unfolds like a flower
In prayer to the warmth of the inner sun.
In each tradition psychic centres catch
Spiritual energy and rotate it,
Translate it by subtle alchemy to
Something golden, admission of the Fire.
So Stauffenberg opened his heart centre,
Received and gave out, in relaxed tension
In a balance between two opposites
That mirrored the light and dark forces that
Hold in relaxed tension the sun and stars.

Just as Dietrich Eckart was mentor to
Hitler, and opened his centres to power,
Demoniac energy from Satan,
So Stefan George was mentor to all three
Stauffenberg brothers, Claus having met him
At sixteen, and been in his circle, drawn
On his symbolist poetry, his meetings
With Mallarmé and with Rudolf Steiner
And members of the Golden Dawn. George's
Pythagorean circle of Truth stressed
Nobility, discipline, sacrifice –
And Light. In poems like *Introit* George
Described an avatar of the arcane
In terms of darkness and of "inmost blaze",
And in his *Secret Germany* "the flame
On his cheek". He read poems with incense
Burning, as a ritual that symbolised
Harmony with the divine, inner strength,
The esoteric Light that stood against
"The Prince of Vermin" of his *Antichrist*,
Hitler himself. George opened Stauffenberg's
Centres to the Light and blended occult
Paganism with Stauffenberg's Catholic
Upbringing, so there was opposition
Between demoniac Hitler and now

Illumined Stauffenberg, whose harmony,
And his brothers', did the will of the Light
Like the thirteenth century Knight of Bamberg,
Shone a radiance into the darkness
And proclaimed the anti-racist outlook
Of Barbarossa's grandson, who entered
Jerusalem like Christ on Palm Sunday
After the Sixth Crusade and was crowned king:
Frederick the Second, the German king and
Holy Roman Emperor who welcomed Jews
And Arabs in his universal state,
His multi-racial court in Sicily.
Berthold and others in George's circle
Had visited his tomb in Palermo
Where he was laid to rest in twelve fifty.

Having visited Heisenberg, Christ joined
The two Stauffenberg brothers in Wannsee,
Where Heydrich had held the conference that
Set the Final Solution on the Jews.
Claus Stauffenberg had been summoned to the
Wolf's Lair, Rastenburg. His brother Berthold
Said, "We must go ahead for the sake of
Our country and our children." They wanted
Rommel, the most admired General at home,
Whose popularity could end the war
And present surrender to the people,
To be the new Head of State. Claus travelled
With Fromm, his Commander. At the Wolf's Lair
There was rebuilding as the HQ had
Only moved back the previous day, and there
Was no chance to explode the bomb. Satan,
Whose spies had found out what was intended,
Lodged a thought in Hitler's mind to change rooms
And have security checks on cases,
And Christ, loitering unseen by Satan,
Could not bring Claus and his bomb near Hitler.
In Berlin, the operation began
To take over Germany, "Valkyrie",
And passed off as an exercise. Depressed,
Claus rang his wife in Bamberg and asked her
To postpone a visit with their children
To family at Lautlingen, but she
Had already bought the railway tickets.
Claus and his brother, exhausted, met in

Wannsee with Quirnheim, Schulenburg and Solz,
Wartenburg, Hofacker, Schwanenfeld and
Hansen. Rommel had sent a message to
Kluge and Hitler that the western front
Could only hold out twenty-one more days.
Christ sat with them, invisible, and poured
Into their minds a thought, and then heard them
Agree to kill Hitler and make peace with
The USSR and western Allies,
Not knowing that they had already cut
Germany up among themselves. Christ heard.

At Blay on July the sixteenth General
Browning, Commander of all the airborne
Divisions told Montgomery, "We've found
Rommel's HQ, and know where he goes to
Fish and shoot pigeons. The SAS could
Try to capture him, but that could just prove
Risky and might fail. Would you like us to
Kill him?" Montgomery started, as if
His deepest thoughts had been externalised.
Which was right? To say Yes, which would help him
Break out of Normandy, or say No as
A Christian? Montgomery knew what prayer
Would say, but he needed a success to
Report to Eisenhower. He wanted war
To be like a duel fought fairly between
Two gentlemen with a code, but fair play
Had no place in war. Capturing Rommel
Would be difficult, it was safer to
Kill him. Montgomery went to the Light
And asked forgiveness for what he must say.
He pondered while Michael, huge at his side,
Aghast, did nothing to influence him,
Knowing that his adversary should not
Be removed from this theatre of the war
So soon before Count Stauffenberg's attempt
To end the war with German surrender,
Which needed a popular General to
Persuade the people to accept the plan;
But wanting Rommel off the battlefield.
Michael dithered, and without clear guidance
Montgomery saw from his perspective,
Not that of the more reliable Whole.
"Yes," he said to Browning, Du Maurier's

Husband, whose daughter Tessa would marry
His own son David, who would be friends with
Rommel's son Manfred and read lessons with
Him in church at soldiers' reunions.

Rommel was in his staff car on a road
Near Livarot with two staff officers,
A driver and a sentry in the back.
At six p.m. two Allied planes swooped down
On the orders of Browning, confirmed on
The previous night by Montgomery,
And strafed him. His driver was killed, Rommel
Was thrown out of the car unconscious with
His staff officers and air sentry, and
Taken to Ste Foy de Montgomery,
The nearest village, seat of the forebears
Of General Montgomery, then Bernay,
Where he was found to have a fractured skull
And wounds to his temple. He could not now
Be Head of State in Stauffenberg's regime,
A post he did not seek, true to his oath
Of personal loyalty to Hitler,
Sworn to serve, not kill him. Von Kluge took
Over Army Group B himself, combined
The roles of Rommel and Rundstedt, but this
Change of command did not stop the Allies.
When he heard news of Rommel's injuries,
Montgomery was very quiet, brooding
On how fate struck him down in a village
Which bore his own name, after his consent
To the attack. He removed Rommel's framed
Portrait that hung on his caravan wall.

Orders came for Stauffenberg to report
To the Wolf's Lair again. He worked in the
Bendlerblock, Bendlerstrasse, until eight,
Then left to be driven home. He stopped at
A small church in a Berlin suburb, the
Brick Dahlem church (circa twelve twenty) – he
Came from a Catholic family, his
Mother being a Catholic convert – and
Stood alone at the back while Mass was held,
A one-armed, one-eyed man with great bearing.
He prayed: "O Christ, intermediary
Between me and God, please forgive me for

The sin I must commit, to take a life
And endanger the lives of officers.
For nine months I have plotted to restore
Germany's greatness from a tarnished man.
Hitler, Himmler, Göring and Goebbels have
Brought shame to Germany, killing millions,
Fighting needlessly with the Soviets,
Spreading senseless destruction on our east
And west flanks, and misery through the world.
O Christ, I have a wife who is pregnant
And four small children, and two brothers – please
Protect them all. I do not want to put
Them at risk, endanger my family,
But I must do this, commit this great sin.
Judge me by my intentions – if by my
Bald deeds alone, then I am doomed to Hell,
To damnation. Yet if *that* is the price,
I must still commit this sin, kill Hitler,
For I must rid the earth of a vileness
And leave your universe a better place."
And then he felt he was not alone now,
He felt Christ beside him, and heard him say,
"Claus, you are right to do tomorrow what
You planned to do. I am with you. Hitler
Is a scourge on mankind, the only way
To free man is to take sinful action.
Claus, your sin is forgiven, for I can see
The nobility in your heart. You are
One of my saints, your sacrifice will be
Remembered as long as time. Claus, be strong."
Stauffenberg, praying, felt a surge of power
And, serene, peaceful in the Light, he glowed.

The next morning, July the twentieth,
The day of destiny, the planned for day,
Stauffenberg left his apartment at six.
His brother drove him to Rangsdorf airfield
Where he met Haeften and Stieff. They flew at
Eight and arrived at Rastenburg at ten-
Fifteen. He left Haeften in charge of his
Briefcase with two two-pound packages of
A sealed plastic explosive, hexogen.
He was to confer with Buhle and Keitel,
Then report on new reserve home units.
At Hitler's situation conference

Which had been brought forward to twelve-thirty
Because Mussolini was arriving.
He had been summoned to give his report.
That summer day was hot and airless, and,
After a breakfast under an oak-tree
And long meetings in Jodl's house and then
In Keitel's bunker, Keitel announced that
Hitler's conference was moved from his closed
Bunker to a wooden building, the Map
Or Operations Room at the Wolf's Lair:
A tall-gabled chalet with neat windows
Surrounded by tall trees, set in a wood.
Stauffenberg asked to wash and change his shirt,
And was shown to a nearby private room.
He came out to where Haeften sat, guarding
Two two-pound packages of explosive.
He planned to use both, and with bent pincers
Held between his left thumb and two fingers
He broke the fuse capsule on one package,
Setting the silent ten-minute long fuse.
Observing, Satan, with skilled mind-control,
Influenced Keitel and a nearby guard.
The door opened, an orderly said that
Keitel wanted him to hurry up, and
Keitel's adjutant called, "Do come along,
Now." In haste Stauffenberg closed the briefcase.
Haeften said, "You've only used one package."
Stauffenberg said, "It will be enough," and
Hurriedly left the room, walked to the hut,
Handed the briefcase to the adjutant
And said, "Place me close to the Führer so
I can hear the discussion as I have
Impaired hearing." Freyend put him two down
From Hitler's right, where all were standing round
A map table. He put the briefcase down.
In the room respectfully round Hitler
Stood sixteen military men, two SS
Officers – Gunsche and Fegelein – and
Two shorthand writers and Sonnleithner, who
Was Ribbentrop's liaison official.
On cue Haeften said, "Phone call from Berlin."
Hanging his cap and belt in the entrance
Stauffenberg left and stood with Fellgiebel.
They got into a car they had ordered
And watched. Satan lurked near open windows,

Appalled, and, disguised as a Nazi in
Uniform, sent a telepathic thought
At mind-control frequency to Colonel
Brandt, who bent and moved the briefcase aside.
Standing near the door, Michael did not see,
Nor did Christ, who sat near Stauffenberg's arm,
Beside him in his hour of trial, giving
Him strength. There was a long silence as good
And evil forces poured into men in
And outside the gabled hut. Then there was
A bright yellow flash and a deafening
Thud and bits of wood flew from the window
As those inside were flung down, burned, bruised and
Pierced by splinters. Two seemingly lifeless
Bodies were thrown out. Stauffenberg and his
Aide Fellgiebel drove by and saw a huge
Cloud of black smoke and dust, and as klaxons
Blared phones began to ring and first aid men
Ran to and fro. Count Stauffenberg said, "No
One could have survived that blast." They drove to
The first check-point, and bluffed through, but the south
Guardhouse had closed the outer gate, and the
Military guard refused to let them through.
Stauffenberg telephoned Möllendorf, one
Of the HQ Commandant's officers,
Who ordered the guard to let them both pass.
Haeften threw the sealed hexogen package
Out of the car window into the woods.
They drove to the airfield where a Heinkel
Waited, its engines running; like a fly
On a table, twitching its legs and wings.
Capless, Stauffenberg half-ran. They clambered
On board and took off for Berlin, convinced
That they had struck the blow to end the war.

The hut was wrecked. The windows were blown out,
The blast went with them, and as the smoke cleared
The damage was less than it would have been
If the blast had blown back from concrete walls.
Hitler lay by the door under timbers
From the ceiling, his hair and clothes on fire,
His right elbow hurting, his eyes smarting,
Seeing contorted screams, choking from fumes.
He stood, beat out the flames on his trousers.
It appeared that he was not badly hurt,

Being protected by the oak table
Which he had leaned across, magnifying
Glass in left hand, coloured pencils in right.
It had massive oak legs. Four men seemed dead.
Most suffered burst eardrums. From crossed timbers
Keitel rose and embraced Hitler, saying,
"My Führer, you're alive! You are alive!"
Most scrambled to their feet and stumbled out,
Some climbed through windows, dazed, cut, unsteady.
Shaken, with a smoke-blackened face, grim but
Unscathed, Hitler had burns, splinters, a bruise,
Torn skin. His trousers were in shreds, his hair
Singed from the fire. He left the room and went
Into the Guest Bunker to change, and said,
"I thought it might be a paratroop raid
So I avoided the windows." Keitel
Said, "It must have been a Todt workman." But
Hitler said, "A German workman would not
Lift his hand against me. This is Army,
General Staff, I have sensed opposition.
They are cowards, they did not dare pull out
A gun and risk their own lives. I will soon
Make an example of them, for they have
Raised their hands against the German State in
Wartime. They must be executed, all."
To his secretaries he said, "Ladies, things
Have turned out well again, I'm glad to say."
And when Dr. Morell arrived, he crowed,
"I am invulnerable, immortal.
My enemies can't blow me up, for I
Am indestructible. My survival
Is a great miracle. I am unharmed,
I am divinely protected. This is
The greatest miracle." Dr. Morell
Took Hitler's pulse, which was seventy-two,
And found torn skin on his legs, a rear raw
As a baboon's. A hundred splinters pierced
His skin, a timber had bruised his forehead.
There was slight bleeding in his deafened ears.
After first aid for minor cuts and burns
Hitler emerged alive, awesome, unmoved.

General Fellgiebel stood outside the Guest
Bunker, waiting for news of Hitler. When
He saw him, he congratulated him

At once on his survival instead of
Shooting him to complete the plot, and said
To Jodl, "We are too near the front line."
Jodl said, "HQ is a building site,"
Meaning a Communist worker had placed
The bomb. Then Stauffenberg's disappearance
Was noticed. Before one, Fellgiebel rang
His Chief of Staff at Mauerwald and said,
"Something terrible has happened. Listen,
The Führer's alive! Get a message to
The Bendlerstrasse." Fellgiebel blocked all
Telecommunication messages
Until the switchboard stopped outgoing calls
Except for Hitler's, Keitel's and Jodl's.

Standing aghast near the Guest Bunker, Christ,
Unseen, saw Satan's jubilation at
Hitler's survival, and knew Hitler was
Surrounded by a wall of dark, and was
Too well protected by infernal powers
For human agency to take his life.
And as God had allocated control
Over matter to the dark force and did
Not interfere, like a President who
Delegates and accepts the outcome though
It is not to his liking, there was no
More that could now be done. It is outside
The power of the Light force to destroy, Love
Creates and grows all spirits free from all
But thought, and that is merely suggestion,
Not coercion. Spirits choose when to leave
Their bodies and return to Heaven or Hell,
To light or dark, and only humans and
Demons can malevolently kill. With
A heavy heart, Christ turned away, knowing
His plan, approved by the Angels, had failed
For now all Nazis wished to appear loyal;
That the war was not over, and many
Millions would now die from the Russian and
Allied advances and air offensives,
In occupied countries, in death camps, from
Buzz-bombs and new weapons; that the death toll
Of the last five years, twenty-five million,
Would be exceeded in the next few months.
Another thirty million would now die,

And had Hitler died in the Guest Bunker
The casualties in the war could have been
Halved. Tears filled his unseen eyes for he knew
That Love was now in conflict with dire Hate,
That he had needlessly caused great hurt to
A shorthand writer and three officers
Who, though Nazi, he must admit to Heaven;
And that nothing could stop a Hellish purge
Of the Germans who most loved what is good.
He may have slowed the German atom bomb
But not infernal genocide of Jews,
And the price of his failure was thirty
Million souls who would die a violent death.
Christ was depressed, and withdrew to the woods.

At two-thirty Mussolini arrived.
When Mussolini was overthrown by
Marshal Badoglio, a Freemason,
The previous July, and imprisoned,
Hitler had sent SS Colonel Otto
Skorzeny to free him and bring him back
To Germany as the Führer's guest. Now
Hitler greeted him as he left his train,
"Duce, I have just had a stroke of good
Fortune." He took the Duce to his Lair,
Which armoured vehicles now ringed in the woods,
And showed him the wrecked hut, the fallen beams.
Bormann, eager to ingratiate, brought
Him the corporal who stood by the hut phone.
He briefly heard the corporal describe
How a one-armed Colonel had hurried off
Without his cap, belt or briefcase. Army
Officers defended Stauffenberg, but
Gestapo investigators found shreds
Of his yellow briefcase in the wrecked hut.
In the tea house, Hitler spoke with his guest,
He explained to the Duce how Speer was
Producing tanks, guns and ammunition,
And how he had a new weapon, V-2,
That would blitz and "raze London to the ground".
At four Fromm telephoned Keitel and said,
"There are rumours here in Berlin that the
Führer is dead, should I declare a state
Of emergency?" "The Führer's alive!"
Keitel bellowed. "There is no cause for that.

Is Stauffenberg in Berlin?" Fromm stammered,
"No, I thought he was with you." The Wolf's Lair,
Which received all orders to the commands,
Then monitored orders from Fromm's office,
Proclaiming a state of emergency,
Codenamed "Valkyrie", appointing Rundstedt's
Predecessor, Field Marshal Witzleben
Supreme Commander of the Wehrmacht and
Hoepner Commander of the Home Forces.
Hitler now grasped a coup was in progress,
Made Himmler his successor and gave his
Gestapo powers to arrest officers
Of the Army. Himmler left for Berlin,
Keitel sent messages to the commands:
"Do not obey orders from General Fromm."

Stauffenberg arrived in the Bendlerblock
At three-thirty to find confusion. There
Was doubt that Hitler was dead, "Valkyrie"
Had not been set in motion: Fellgiebel's
Message was relayed to Olbricht, who did
Nothing, not sure if Hitler was dead, and
Unwilling to start a coup. Stauffenberg
Took charge, assuring all Hitler was dead,
Bluffing so as to keep the coup going,
Convincing them he had seen Hitler's corpse,
Galvanising the officers. Quirnheim
Sent out messages, saying the Army
Had taken over, under General Beck.
After his call to Keitel, Fromm refused
To co-operate with the coup, despite
Stauffenberg's urgings. The one-armed man said,
"Field Marshal Keitel is lying. Why, I
Saw Hitler's body being carried out.
The explosion was as if the hut had
Been hit by a six-inch shell. No one who
Was in that room can still be alive now."
Olbricht said, "The orders for Valkyrie
Have been given." Fromm rose from his desk, banged
His fists and raged, "I am in command here,
I will not allow my subordinates
To do such things. You are all guilty of
Insubordination, revolution,
Treason. The penalty for all of you
Is death. Who gave the orders?" Olbricht said,

"Colonel Mertz von Quirnheim." Quirnheim came in,
Asked to confirm this he said, "Yes, I did."
Fromm spoke: "You are all now under arrest.
Quirnheim, cancel the orders." Quirnheim sat
And said, "Colonel-General, since I am
Under arrest, my freedom of movement
Is restricted." Fromm said, "The attempted
Assassination has failed. Stauffenberg,
You will have no alternative but to
Shoot yourself." Stauffenberg said, "No, *we* are
In control, you are deluded for *you*
Are under arrest." Fromm rose from his desk
And lunged at Stauffenberg with flailing fists,
Shouting, "You haven't been my Chief of Staff
Three weeks, and now you're getting me into
Trouble with the Führer. It is monstrous."
But Haeften and Kleist drew their pistols and
Took Fromm's pistol and shut him in the room
Of his own adjutant Bartram next door
Under guard. After six Fellgiebel rang:
"Are you all crazy? The Führer is now
With the Duce in the tea room there will
Be a radio communiqué soon."

General von Hase, Berlin's Commandant,
Had failed to take control of the city,
But had told Major Remer to cordon
Off the government quarter and arrest
All Nazis as Hitler was dead. One of
Goebbels' propaganda staff, Hans Hagen,
Was lecturing to Remer's officers,
And, suspecting a coup, told Remer, "It would
Be advisable to tell Goebbels." He
Left, and Remer's troops climbed into vehicles.
Remer reported to Hase and heard
Two men order the arrest of Goebbels.
He frowned, loyal to Hase and Hitler.

Goebbels, in his Propaganda office
With Speer and Funk, heard from Hagen and saw
Remer's troops surrounding the building. Then
Hitler phoned. Loyal Goebbels said, "Führer,
A failed assassination attempt? That
Is scandalous, treasonous, criminal.
You are safe. That is Providential. Yes,

A coup is in progress, my Ministry
Is being surrounded. I'll deal with it."
He pocketed some capsules of poison
And sent for Remer, who, reaching his door,
Now said, "Sir, I have orders. The Führer
Has been assassinated, the SS
Are attempting a putsch, I must seal off
The Wilhelmstrasse and arrest certain
Ministers, including you."
Goebbels thought
Quickly. He said, "But you have an oath of
Personal loyalty to the Führer."
Remer said, "The Führer is dead." Goebbels
Said, "He's alive, a group of ambitious
Generals has begun a putsch, the dirtiest
In history. I will speak to the Führer.
You will speak to him." Loyal Goebbels rang
Hitler and said, "I have Major Remer
Here." He passed the phone to Remer who clicked
His heels and barked "Jahwohl, mein Führer" as
Hitler said: "You have full authority
To take all measures, however drastic,
To save the government of the Reich, and
You are now promoted Colonel. You will
Obey my orders or those of Himmler,
Who is Commander of Reserve Army
In place of Fromm. Crush the rebellion in
Berlin, arrest the plotters. I'll broadcast
That the coup has failed." Remer stood transfixed,
And with a final "Jahwohl, mein Führer"
He left with Goebbels for his headquarters
And took his troops to Goebbels's garden
In Hermann-Göring-Strasse, where Goebbels
Addressed them. Remer sent Gehrke to a
Panzer unit under Guderian
And kept them loyal. Then he sent Schlee to
The Bendlerblock to cordon the building.
Schlee slipped in and encountered Quirnheim, who
Forbad him to leave. He slipped out again,
And told Remer there was a putsch being
Run from the Bendlerblock, which was its nest.
Remer sent Schady to surround the block
And to arrest all Generals found inside.

Inside the Bendlerblock Stauffenberg saw

Troops outside. He knew he was surrounded.
Exhausted, he took off his black eye patch,
And sat, fatigued and frustrated, near Beck.
In Paris his cousin Hofacker had,
With his superior Stülpnagel, made
Arrests in the SS. Stülpnagel had
Gone to La Roche Guyon with Horst, Speidel's
Brother-in-law, and Hofacker. Kluge,
Who after Rommel's wounding commanded
Army Group B, pulled away from the plot.
Depressed, Stauffenberg soldiered on. And then
At ten-thirty gunfire echoed inside
The Army building. Schlee had now returned
With soldiers, Gehrke brought more. They freed Fromm
And two more Nazis under guard, Kortzfleisch
And Pifrader and his aide, who had come.
Stauffenberg hurried down a corridor
Towards the sound. A crack behind him, pain
As a bullet tore through his left shoulder,
The shoulder of his good arm and one hand.
Other plotters rushed to his aid, more shots
Were fired. Stauffenberg, bleeding profusely,
Was supported by the plotters into
Fromm's office, where, released, Fromm now joined them.
Haeften drew his pistol, Fromm cringed, cowered.
Stauffenberg, still bleeding, stood erect and
Gave Fromm a withering look of contempt
And gestured that Haeften should drop his gun.
He was an honourable man who lived
By a strict code that excluded revenge.

Fromm stood before the six men with Gehrke,
Having to show he was on Hitler's side.
They could speak of his own involvement in
The plot and they had to die before they
Could be questioned by the Gestapo. He
Declared, "I have convened a court martial."
Five remained defiant. Stauffenberg said,
"He has known of the plot for weeks and has
Done nothing to prevent it and he wants
To kill us so we can't reveal that he
Is one of us. And now he is our judge
And jury. Some trial." Fromm barked, "Quiet. You will
Not speak unless spoken to." He said, "I

Pronounce you guilty of conspiring to
Assassinate our Führer, high treason.
General Beck, General Olbricht, Colonel-
General Mertz, this Colonel whose name I will
Not speak, Lieutenant-General Hoepner and
Lieutenant von Haeften are condemned to
Death. Sentence will be carried out at once.
Have you any last wishes?" Stauffenberg,
Still bleeding, spoke: "I am responsible
For everything. These men were just soldiers
Who obeyed my orders. They are guiltless."
Fromm contradicted, "No, they are guilty."
Beck said, "I wish to keep my pistol for
Private use." Fromm nodded and said, "You must
Do it immediately here in this room."
Stunned at the sudden nearness of his death,
Beck said goodbye, and pointed his Luger
At his temple and pulled the trigger. He
Must have flinched, for he fell wounded into
The bloodstained arm of Stauffenberg. Beck moaned
"Another gun", and a staff officer
Gave him a Mauser. He fired again but
Only fell. He lay moaning on the floor.
Fromm said full of contempt, "He has even
Bungled that. Please help the old gentleman."
A sergeant gave him the coup de grâce. Bits
Of brain spattered the wall and floor, and the
Grim-faced plotters averted their eyes and
Winced. Fromm said, "Take his leather overcoat
As your reward. Have you any more last
Wishes?" Hoepner, who had been Fromm's close friend,
Said, "I had nothing to do with the plot,
I wish to compose a defence." Olbricht
Said, "I wish to write a statement." Fromm thought,
Then nodded. For half an hour Olbricht wrote
While Stauffenberg sat quietly in the Light,
Eyes closed, removed from his body, aware
Of Christ beside him in his hour of trial,
His crucifixion and self-sacrifice,
Thinking of his wife and four children and
Praying Hitler would not execute them;
While Hoepner persuaded his friend Fromm to
Talk in private. He was placed in a room
Apart from the others, under arrest,
Pending investigation. Then Fromm heard

That Guard Battalion troops under Schady
Had arrived. He ordered his adjutant
Bartram to pick ten NCOs and line
Them all up in the courtyard in front of
A pile of sand left over from building
Work. At midnight Fromm said, "Take these four down."
Under armed guard and calm, bold Stauffenberg
Said, "We will rise above their guns and hold
Ourselves erect, for our humane idea
Was right. What we thought we will act, our self-
Control will show we still hold our beliefs,
Our stance of mastery in the face of
Wrong. We will call others to complete our
Task. Goodbye my loyal friends." And then he,
Olbricht, Haeften and Quirnheim were marched down
The stone stairs to the double doorway and
Out into the cobbled courtyard now lit
By hooded headlights of lined army trucks.
They stood before the pile of sand, showing
No emotion. Ten Unteroffizieren
Took aim, ghostly figures in the headlights.
Stauffenberg, still bleeding from his shoulder,
Shouted, "Long live Sacred Germany," and
Some thought he shouted "Secret Germany",
The title of Stefan George's poem,
Fulfilling his oath of allegiance to
George's ideals that lay behind his coup,
Of discipline, sacrifice and freedom,
Of Light. And as the volley crashed Haeften
Flung himself in front of Stauffenberg and
Took his bullets. Three bodies lay; bleeding,
Stauffenberg still stood, proud, defiant and
Almost at prayer as, with closed eyes, he looked
For the Light that had guided him, serene,
A one-armed, one-eyed, bleeding man who stood
Against Hitler – and now fell on the sand,
Slowly toppling like a tall poplar tree
When felled by woodsmen who cut out a wedge,
As a new volley rang round the courtyard.

The four bodies were driven to a churchyard
And immediately buried. Fromm sent
A teleprinter message to Hitler:
"Attempted putsch by irresponsible
Generals bloodily crushed. All ringleaders

Shot." Soon after, Speer and Remer arrived.
Fromm told them, "I've just had some criminals
Executed." Remer was not pleased, he
Wanted to question the four men. He told
Fromm to accompany him for questioning
By Goebbels and Himmler, which took place in
The Propaganda Ministry over
Brandy and cigars. Fromm declared he had
Shot the four out of loyalty. Later
He was arrested – he had not deceived
Hitler – and tried and shot "for cowardice",
For not doing enough to stop the plot.

At 1 a.m. after martial music
Hitler's voice crackled on German wireless:
"I am speaking to you so you may know
I am unhurt and well, and so you may
Hear details of a crime unparalleled
In German history. A conspiracy
To eliminate me has been hatched by
A tiny clique of ambitious, stupid,
Irresponsible and criminal men,
Officers of our Army. I was spared
A fate which holds no terror for me, but
Would have had terrible consequences
For the German people. I regard this
As a sign that I should now continue
The task imposed on me by Providence.
The criminals will all be ruthlessly
Exterminated." A shudder swept through
The German people for they knew a purge
Of terrifying savagery would now
Destroy battalions of the virtuous
And good. They knew no one was safe. Despite
The noble stance of Stauffenberg, it seemed
He had set off a wave of terror that
Would engulf his colleagues and family,
Set back the cause of surrender and peace.

Human perspective differs from divine
As ground views differ from aerial photos
Or present time does from the whole process,
The pattern by which past becomes future.
It seemed to Stauffenberg in his present,
In the Bendlerstrasse, that he must stop

The war to prevent millions more deaths and
Atrocities, and he was right that there
Would be more. But God, seeing from a whole
Perspective, how present disasters shaped
The future, required cruel events that
Would change the pattern from domination
By Nazis to Soviet-Allied conflict,
To opposites that, eventually,
Could merge in harmony and, reconciled,
Bring in global unity, destroying
The old. It was necessary Hitler
Should be stung into a further onslaught
On humankind, so that his regime could
Be shaken like a kaleidoscope and
Fall into a pattern of opposites
From which a New World Order could emerge.
So, though it seemed that Stauffenberg had lost,
That Hitler had triumphed to kill and maim,
In fact he damaged Hitler just enough
To advance God's will through increased terror
For long enough to ensure his slaughter
Of Russians and Jews would draw the Russians
Towards Eastern Europe, Jews to Israel,
While all spirits released from life would be
Reborn into a far better pattern.
So Satan, thinking he was triumphing,
Believing he thwarted the work of God,
Without realising it performed God's will.

Being is more bright, less dense than this world
Of Becoming and its earth-energy,
And though there appear to be two forces,
One Fire, one Dark, around the windswept earth
Like a sea's leaping light and windstruck rock,
There is ultimately, beyond conflict,
One force that shows itself both bright and dark
As the electro-magnetic spectrum
Has dense low frequencies and gamma rays,
Or as a rainbow has bright and dark bands.
Dark contained the First Cause, potential Fire,
Which contained denser Dark, shone through by Light;
Both forces – all things – manifested from
The One and are two currents within one
Energy, one subtle, one dense. And so,
Like an ocean round the earth, one power

Swirls and we sea-sponges are filled with Light
Or Dark tides, depending on how wise and
Porous our souls are, or how dense and coarse.
What seems two is one, yet is seen as two,
For ignorance is not knowledge, and sees
Itself as being apart from gnosis
Of its own source, to which it must return
To dwell within the Light or, beyond its
Margin, in grim separation, in Hell.
And Heaven and Hell, though they appear as two,
Are likewise one spectrum from fine to dense,
From knowledge to deceiving ignorance.
So though Stauffenberg knew Light of Being
Which pours round the earth like a gentle sea,
Hitler knew a chthonic power, a dense force
That hugs ley lines, galvanises matter
Like electricity, blows like the wind.
And though, like winds and tides, both are aspects
Of the One spectrum like Light and lightning,
They are as separate as spiritual
Christ is from deliberately carnal
Satan, god of matter and flesh and sex
Whose consciousness is denser than Christ's love,
Is self-interested and not selfless,
Of the physical ego, not the soul,
Of the reason, not the intuition,
On Landulf's side, not Frederick the Second's.
Good and evil are two strong currents in
The same flowing tide that foams round the earth,
One in bright calm, one on the wind-whipped top,
One twinkling light, and one dense surf and froth.
One fills soul-makers, one lost souls with power.

The universe is governed by two laws
Which are opposing forces held at one:
The expanding Fire and speed Hubble found
That counteracts gravity as Newton
Thought, and spits out galaxies like bonfire
Sparks; and the contracting Darkness and wreck
Of decaying Dark Matter and black holes,
Destruction and evil – like the black hole
V404 Cygni six thousand light
Years away which is swallowing a star
Nearly as large as our sun, whose weight it
Exceeds twelve times, and is so massive that

Nothing, not even light, can escape from
Its gravitational pull, and devours
Any thing that comes close enough to it,
And leaves no trace of what it has eaten.
Each force has its own law, and each one has
Its time. Look at expansion, and the age
Of the universe is sixteen billion
Years; (and the most distant galaxy known
As 8C 1435 + 63
Is fifteen billion light years away, and
Contains stars that were old when their light set
Out); look at decomposition – the stars –
And the age is eight to twelve billion years.
Time is many sequences of events.
Out of white holes (one near this earth) pours stuff,
As from a Roman cornucopia;
Into black holes like drains stuff disappears.
Both forces are in balance, birth and death,
New and old, light and dark, plus and minus.
God the zero Fire holds all opposites:
Zero equals plus A plus minus A
(O = (+A) + (-A)),
The universe both expands and contracts
And thrives on the tension between forces,
The balance Newton sought and Einstein found
(The cosmological constant), and then
Doubted, the tension that balanced Hitler
And brave Stauffenberg, who was cheered in Heaven;
Nazi tyranny and brave Eisenhower
Despairing at Montgomery's slowness,
Moving his headquarters to Normandy.
God is Cosmic Christ plus Cosmic Satan.
God, Fire, contains what reason separates,
Making one two, truth into illusion,
Reducing the whole to conflicting parts,
Laws, forces, Heaven, Hell, Christ and Satan,
The sea to eddying currents and tides,
A multiplicity of opposites
Which intuition restores to a whole,
Seeing all division is of the One.
God, Fire, shows difference is deception
And unites and blends the Darkness and Light.
God, Fire, includes the Darkness and the Light.

Printed in the United States
5063